PANTHER

DAVID OWEN

ATOM

ATOM

First published in Great Britain in 2015 by Corsair
This edition published in 2016 by Atom

13 5 7 9 10 8 6 4 2

A CIP catalogue record for this book is
available from the British Library.

ISBN 978-0-349-002-74-3 (paperback)
ISBN 978-1-47211-643-7 (eBook)

Printed and bound by CPI Group (UK) Ltd, Croydon, CR0 4YY

Papers used by Atom are from well-managed forests and
other responsible sources.

MIX
Paper from
responsible sources
FSC® C104740

Atom
An imprint of
Little, Brown Book Group
Carmelite House
50 Victoria Embankment
London EC4Y 0DZ

An Hachette UK Company
www.hachette.co.uk
www.atombooks.co.uk

For Christina,
the bravest person I know.

Chapter One

The cookie broke apart in his mouth like smashed concrete. It was so stale that his saliva turned it into glue and his teeth stuck together. It didn't matter to Derrick. He forced his jaw to keep working the mouthful until it was soft enough to swallow. It wasn't about the taste. Not after what had happened to him that afternoon. Not when the cookie was days old and scavenged from the dustbin.

He delved his hand back into the bin bag. Cold moisture tingled on his skin as something mushy swamped his fingers. Derrick didn't even flinch. The first time he had ever done this the slightest touch of anything wet had made him whip his hand clear and wipe it frantically on the weeds that grew through the fence. Now he'd done it so many times that nothing would stop him.

Why do you do this? he asked himself. It was a question he could never answer. These eating sprees had only begun a few months back. Since then he'd watched the fat swell under his skin, his belly sag over his waistband. It had only taken a couple of months for him to completely lose control.

That was the funny thing. He ate because everything at home was out of control. He ate because it made him feel *in* control. Even Derrick couldn't figure it out.

The cloying smell of rubbish filled his nose. His hand found another cookie that was too soggy to consider, then another, which just about made the grade. In the darkness it was little more than a disc of shadow between his fingers. Too dark to make out if anything nasty was stuck to it. Derrick shrugged and shoved it into his mouth whole.

It cracked between his teeth. Derrick tipped his head back to the night sky. With each chew he felt the tension ooze out of his body. It felt like his feet were sinking into the earth. The knot of anger in his stomach, pulled so tight that day that he thought it might snap, began to fall slack as the junk food slopped down into his gut.

These days junk food was the only thing that soothed the anger. Even if it was only for a few hours. It had been that way for three months now. Ever since the incident. Ever since Charlotte had tried to kill herself.

A high-pitched yelp echoed across the allotments and chased the memory from his mind. When he was little, he'd always thought that the fox cries were the screams of women in trouble. Back then he would never have gone to the alley at the bottom of the garden after midnight. It was the only way to make sure his family didn't see him raiding the bins for days-old junk food, something he wasn't exactly proud of.

2

Derrick looked down at the bulge of his stomach. The sight of it. This was her fault. It was the only way to cope with everything Charlotte was putting them through.

The fox screamed again, a strangled wail that snapped his thoughts in two. Derrick leaned back against the wooden fence that lined one side of the alley. It formed an uneven black barrier that cut him off from the segmented back gardens that ran the length of the street. The wood creaked under his weight. Just enough dim light filtered through from the surrounding houses for him to pick out the vegetable patches, sheds, wonky frameworks and mismatched garden furniture of the allotments opposite. Three months ago he'd learned the place like the back of his hand. There was no sign of the fox. The only sound now was the low vibration of a helicopter somewhere behind the roofs.

Derrick swallowed the last of the cookie. It wasn't quite enough to push away his worries. Things were only going to get worse from here. Charlotte's final exams were next week. The thought of how the stress might make her behave sent a shiver up his spine. There had already been crying and tantrums. The atmosphere in the house was already becoming too tense to bear.

She couldn't just get on with things like everybody else. His exams were finished and *he'd* got through them fine. Ok, she was a couple of years ahead, hers were probably a bit harder. But that shouldn't be an excuse. Charlotte always made such a big deal out of everything.

3

Depression – Derrick just didn't get it.

He felt his jogging bottoms dig into his skin. They used to be loose. He deployed two fingers to tug his T-shirt (XXL, bought in a charity shop) away from his body.

He wiped crumbs from his mouth. When he had chucked the remains of this food away a couple of days ago, the idea had been to stop himself eating too much. The irony wasn't lost on him. Just like with everything else, he should have known better.

He sighed. *Why do you do this?* On top of what they had caught him doing at school earlier that day, Derrick wondered if he had any pride left at all.

A little way up the alley the chain-link fence that cut him off from the allotments rattled. The sound made his skin prickle. The fence rattled harder, as if someone were shaking it, sending a metallic ripple all the way along to meet the garden gate with a loud *slap-slap-slap*. Somewhere in the thick darkness, something unseen scuffled on the soil.

'Bugger off,' blurted Derrick. He wasn't sure why.

But the noise didn't bugger off and the whole fence rattled like it was going to fall down.

Derrick was pretty sure he should run for it. His feet inched back. It would have taken him maybe fifteen seconds to clear the lawn and reach the back door of the house. That didn't factor in the possibility of getting a stitch and falling over halfway.

Only a single thought made him stand his ground. *What if they're filming you again?*

If they'd caught Derrick eating out of the dustbin,

the video would be on YouTube within the hour. Maybe this was an extra part of the prank. Bonus footage. An extra freak-out to make it really humiliating. As if the video they'd made earlier that day hadn't been humiliating enough.

When the smartphone had appeared over the top of the toilet stall, he'd known straight away who it was. There was no way to get his trousers up in time. The school meatheads had used Tamoor's phone, while he himself hung back. As if that made it less of a betrayal. Tamoor and Derrick used to be best friends. The end of that friendship was something else that had slipped out of his control.

He forced himself forward. There was no way he could let them get away with it again. Not after everything they'd done to him in the last few months. It wasn't as if Tamoor would stop them.

The helicopter was overhead now, the *buzz* of the blades joining in with the rattling of the fence.

Derrick took another step and felt his stomach turn over. Could projectile vomit be used as a weapon? He took his phone out of his pocket. Swiped the screen and thrust it out ahead of him. Sharp white light illuminated the alley and pushed thin, interweaving shadows through the fence onto the grass.

Suddenly the rattling stopped, leaving the thundering chopper, circling.

Derrick held up his phone to inspect a ragged hole, peeled open in the chain-link, just about big enough for a person to squeeze through. A person a little less wide than himself, anyway.

5

Derrick lowered himself down onto his knees and pressed the screen closer. The earth in front of the hole had been scuffed and churned. It was scarred with shallow grooves like claw marks. Derrick plucked something caught on a barb of metal. It was a clump of black fur. Thick but soft, like the coat of an animal.

Bugger. Three months ago he would have given anything to find this . . .

Derrick tucked his phone back into his pocket and heaved himself upright, clutching the tuft.

Blinding light flooded the alley. Derrick threw his arm across his eyes. *Shit.* He thought for a paranoid split-second it was Tamoor and the meatheads. Oh god. Everyone would laugh at him. Again. He was exposed. Slowly, as if accepting his fate, he opened his eyes and squinted up from under his arm.

The helicopter hovered directly above him, pinning him in a beam of brightness that cut him out of the night. They wouldn't go *this* far. This would be a whole new level of trolling. The turbulence of the thundering blades plastered his T-shirt against his skin. Even in his fear he tried to pry it loose.

The light considered him for a few seconds before it seemed to grow bored. It swung lazily across the allotments, flooding the greenhouses with ghostly white and throwing strange, misshapen shadows across the ground. The helicopter turned and buzzed away, illuminating the empty warehouse in the far corner.

Derrick's hair settled messily over his face. A high-pitched ringing tore at his ears. All he could do was stand and watch the helicopter drift away over the allotments. *POLICE*, Derrick read on its side. Eating from his dustbin wasn't a crime, was it? Derrick had always thought of it more as a total moral disgrace.

After a few minutes the spotlight snapped off like a shrug, the helicopter coasted off over London, and the noise bounced and faded into the distance.

Derrick tried to hold his trembling hands steady. The quiet around him now was absolute. The black fur was gone, blown away into the darkness.

Chapter Two

The reflection in the bathroom mirror always made Derrick sigh. It had been a long time since he was happy with what he saw. Occasionally, depending on how much he had eaten the previous day, it wasn't *quite* as cringe-worthy. Even then, though, it was only a case of how close his stomach looked to bursting. Degrees of shame.

Derrick studied his naked reflection. The dustbin cookies were having their revenge. The fold that cut his belly into two distinctive rolls was even deeper than usual, like a trench at the bottom of the ocean. He'd have to try and hide it with the biggest T-shirt he owned.

Derrick poked a finger into his nipple. The flesh swallowed it up to the fingernail. The meatheads at school had yet to reach a consensus opinion about the proper name for a fat boy's breasts. *Man boobs* was a frontrunner, usually shortened to *moobs*. Tamoor, proudly, had come up with *chesticles*.

When they shouted these at him in the PE changing room, Derrick would try and ignore them and do everything he could to stay in control of himself.

Yesterday that had meant going into the toilet stall for a private moment that had not stayed private for very long at all.

It took one deep breath to summon the courage to step onto the scale. As the digital display rushed upwards he let the air out of his lungs. His belly spread to hide his feet. The only way to see the result was to lean forward. After a thoughtful pause to consider his bulk, the display showed 18 stones and 1 pound. Derrick grimaced. It was just below his all-time personal worst, achieved just two weeks before.

The next step was to lose as much of that weight as possible on the toilet. Returning to the scale ten minutes later, he'd cut down to 17 stones and 13 pounds. Derrick stepped off with a nod. It would have to do. This house would never let him get any slimmer.

Derrick thumped down the stairs in the same jogging bottoms he'd worn the night before. An all-black T-shirt billowed around him (XXXL, ordered specially from America). His school uniform was still a crumpled mess on his bedroom floor. If everything went to plan, he wouldn't be needing it.

Steam curled up from a mug clasped in Mum's hands. When he walked into the kitchen she met him with a nod, but didn't move from her position perched on the edge of the counter. Her smart work shirt was rumpled, as if she hadn't had a chance to iron it.

'Uniform's changed a bit, hasn't it?' she said.

Derrick scraped a chair across the pale linoleum floor and tucked himself in underneath the table. 'I have a compelling argument for staying home today.'

'Save it,' said Mum, as she set her mug down on the counter and slung her work ID around her neck. 'For once I agree with you. As it's Friday.'

Derrick grinned. He'd been prepared for a fight.

'But,' Mum said, wagging a finger, 'there's still the matter of talking to your head teacher.'

Derrick's smile vanished and he scowled into the empty cereal bowl in front of him. Of all the conversations he would rather avoid, this was top of the list. Mr Irvine was probably the least frightening teacher in the world. He wore thick-framed glasses to compensate for his baldness. He'd often take them off and chew one of the arms, trying to look stern. It never worked. Tamoor used to say that Mr Irvine was fired from a girls' school for getting a Year Eight pregnant. That probably wasn't true though. Tamoor told a lot of stories like that. Derrick was pretty sure Year Eight girls didn't even get their periods yet. He'd have to remember to Google it later.

Anyway, it didn't matter if he was a scary head teacher or not. Talking about what happened yesterday was pretty much the last thing he wanted to do with *anyone*.

Beneath the table the cat wound herself around his legs. Derrick cast around the table for something sharp to stick into his arm. Just to cause a distraction. Then he remembered.

You shouldn't even think that. It's not something to joke about.

There had been no knives or scissors in the kitchen since the incident. For the last three months every morning involved remembering to grab a knife from Mum's secret stash before going downstairs. That day, like most days, he'd forgotten. A few days ago he'd spread jam on his toast with the edge of his school calculator.

'No time like the present,' said Mum, as she reached for the cordless phone.

'Can we negotiate?'

'Nope.'

Derrick thought about trying to escape. The back door was ajar and morning sun slanted gently across the garden and the allotments behind it. He could make a run for it. But running was hardly his strong suit.

Mum tapped in the number, but left the handset in the cradle. Then she pressed the button for the speaker and the fuzzy sound of ringing filled up the kitchen. Startled, the cat ran out into the hall.

Mum flashed him a wink, and for just a second Derrick felt the panic in his chest subside. Maybe this wouldn't be so bad?

The ringing was broken on the sixth go around.

'Mr Irvine speaking.'

His voice was thick and weary, as if he'd been asleep head down on his desk all night and the phone had disturbed him mid-dream.

'This is Karen Pietersen,' said Mum.

There was a pause, followed by a rustle of paper. Mr Irvine checking his memos, trying to remember who the hell she was. *'Ah, Mrs Pietersen, good morning. I'm glad we have this chance to talk.'*

Mum rolled her eyes at that. Derrick fought to keep

the smile off his face. Even with her in his corner this could not go well. There was no way for him to explain why he had done it. Not a way that they'd understand, anyway.

On the other end of the line Mr Irvine cleared his throat. *'Now, we both know that Derrick is an unpopular child.'*

Mum's eyes flared wide. 'You're on speaker, Mr Irvine.'

A pause followed. The line crackled like burning paper to punctuate the silence.

'I am?'

'Derrick is right here.'

Mr Irvine seemed to choke on his own throat. *'Mrs Pietersen, please take me off speaker.'*

A mischievous grin tugged at Mum's lips. 'I don't think so.'

Derrick clamped his hand over his mouth to smother a laugh. She rarely behaved like this any more. Usually she was too tired in the morning to do anything but snap at him, or sit in the kitchen with her head on the table. The last few months seemed to have drained all the life out of her.

'Very well then,' said Mr Irvine. *'We've all seen the video –'*

The smile dropped off both of their faces.

'I mean to say, we're all aware what occurred yesterday.'

'You mean my son being humiliated on the Internet?'

'That's one side of it, yes.'

'What other side is there, Mr Irvine?'

Derrick flinched at the tone of her voice. It was the

12

same tone she used to take with Dad before he left. The same she'd used with Charlotte in the early days, and now with him when he trod a little too heavily on the invisible eggshells that littered their house. Nothing good ever came after that tone of voice.

'*Mrs Pietersen, I understand that this has been upsetting. The school is well aware that your family is experiencing a difficult time. That is why no further action is being taken against Derrick. But your son has been much more withdrawn than usual in the last few months. This isn't the first time he's misbehaved in a . . . strange manner. Our concern is that this might be his way of acting out.*'

Derrick kept his eyes on the empty cereal bowl in front of him.

It was hard to argue that he'd been caught doing some strange things at school, like sneaking into the staff toilet or locking his PE teacher in the ball cupboard. There wasn't a reason for doing any of it. It was just because he could.

'*Rest assured we're doing everything we can to identify the persons responsible for making and distributing the video.*'

Derrick flicked the edge of the bowl. Mr Irvine made it sound like an expensively shot porno. Anyway, everyone who wasn't a teacher knew who it was.

Tamoor could have stopped the meatheads. He gave up his phone too easily. The meatheads left it to Tamoor to upload the file to YouTube, like a test he had to pass. Derrick had begged him not to, tried to snatch the phone – but Tamoor just held it at arm's-length above his head. He could have sworn Tamoor never used to be that tall.

13

For a second Derrick thought that he might not do it. That their former friendship still meant something. But Tamoor pressed the button and smiled as they all laughed and shoved each other about to celebrate.

'I understand that –' Mr Irvine pauses. *'Am I still on speaker?'*

'Yes.'

'I understand that Derrick is the victim in this. But I must make it absolutely clear that his behaviour is simply not appropriate in school.'

Mum sighed. Her face folded suddenly with tiredness. That was it. The joke was over. It had lasted longer than it usually did. These days it was like she was doing an impression of herself. The ability to laugh and joke was a facade she wore. It would collapse suddenly into exhaustion when she couldn't keep it up any longer.

'I think we can be sure he won't be at it again.'

Derrick flinched and threw her an angry look. She made him sound like a sex pest.

'I'm glad to hear that.'

'Derrick won't be in today.' Mum cut the call before Mr Irvine could protest. 'No wonder that school is failing.'

She leaned forward to grab a box of cereal and shovelled a handful into her mouth. She stood over him while she chewed, crunching loudly. Derrick recognised the 'Mum Pause' – those seconds she always took to prepare herself to steer the conversation in a serious direction.

'It was Tamoor, wasn't it?'

14

Derrick kept his eyes on the table. 'Don't know.'

'You never did tell me what happened between you two.'

Derrick flicked the bowl again, harder. He didn't know what to tell her. That his best friend – his *only* friend – had ditched him as soon as he found out what happened with Charlotte? Derrick remembered the look on his face when he'd told him. He'd looked at Derrick like he was some kind of weirdo. Like it was some kind of disease that he might catch. It freaked Tamoor out. He knew it did. It was Charlotte's fault. But there was no way Mum would believe that. She'd take Charlotte's side, just like always.

So all Derrick gave her was a shrug.

Mum sighed. 'I still don't understand why you did it in the first place.'

For just a second Derrick thought about trying to explain it. But he knew that she would never understand.

There was no good explanation for his need to do it right at that moment, in the middle of a school day, locked away inside a toilet cubicle. He should have just ignored their insults and got dressed as quickly as possible.

Derrick knew that it was about control. That part of him, making that choice . . . it was one of the only things left in his life that he *could* control.

'Don't tell Dad,' he said.

'I'm hardly in the habit of speaking to your father. But I could really do without this right now, Derrick. Things are hard enough with your sister.'

He brought his hand down hard on the table. The cereal bowl rattled. The air seemed to grow thick at the mention of her. The only important thing in the house was Charlotte. It didn't matter what else was going on. She was all they were supposed to care about now. It felt like they were sealed off from the rest of the world, like there was an invisible barrier on every door and window. The house was slowly filling up with darkness, and there was nothing they could do to escape it.

Derrick looked up at Mum. Her clothes hung off her now. The patches under her eyes were so severe that they looked drawn on with a marker pen. Charlotte was holding them hostage. The whole family was hostage to her depression.

Everything that had gone wrong in this family was her fault. And Derrick didn't know how he could stop it.

'I take it she's not feeling well again today?' said Derrick.

Mum answered with a weary look. 'You know that's not fair.'

'It never is.'

Mum sighed – something she did a lot now – and checked her watch. 'I can't be late again. Just look after your sister for me, ok?'

Before he could answer she kissed him on the head and trotted for the door.

After breakfast he went upstairs and hovered on the landing, listening for any sign of movement from

Charlotte's room. Only when he was satisfied that the coast was clear did he go into Mum's bedroom. The wardrobe was tucked in beside the window, which offered up the clearest view of the allotments from the house.

The space looked smaller in the daylight. The vegetable patches and greenhouses seemed more crammed together. A bright red kiddie swing rocked gently in the morning breeze. Near the back fence, where it was smothered by bushes and long grass, a fox trotted towards the oak tree that towered over everything.

It could have been fox hair he'd found caught in the fence last night. No, it would have been coarse and orange. Anyway, a fox could have made it through that hole without touching the sides.

Derrick opened the wardrobe and peeled back a stack of pillow cases on the bottom shelf. Arranged underneath, like a secret arsenal in a Bond movie, were all the knives from the kitchen. Even plastic ones. They were joined by a couple of pairs of scissors and the rusty saw from the toolkit. Stacked behind them was all the medication in the house, from plain bottles of old prescription tablets through to colourful off-the-shelf hay fever treatments. Mum wasn't taking any chances. Not after last time.

The other side of the wardrobe was being used as storage for all the household junk Charlotte would take to university. There were socks folded inside a frying pan, fresh hand towels, a pack of coat hangers.

Derrick stared at the contraband shoved in alongside all the stuff that would clutter Charlotte's future. Slowly, he wrapped his fingers around the handle of the biggest kitchen knife. He pressed his thumb gently against the blade. How hard would he need to push for it to bite into his skin? The thought made him shudder.

When he opened his laptop, Facebook threatened him with fifteen notifications. Slumped back on his bed, the computer wedged into his belly, he was almost too scared to click. Even though no one at school cared about his existence, they'd still added him online. Derrick could hardly criticise. He'd accepted every request just so that he could pretend to be popular.

Most of the notifications were timeline posts from the night before. All of them were about as witty as Derrick anticipated. There was a reason he'd turned off notifications on his phone.

Hope youve washed ur hands!!

Batty boy!

Someone had posted a link to the video, but it was already disabled. Maybe Tamoor took the video down when the school started paying attention. He'd always avoided trouble if he could.

One of the posts simply said: *WANKER*.

Derrick scrolled down the page without even bothering to notice who had written each comment. It didn't make any difference. The only advantage of going to an all-boys school was that there were no girls to make his embarrassment even worse. The disadvantage was that everyone would definitely now think he was gay.

That didn't really matter though. There was only one girl Derrick cared about seeing it. All he could do

18

now was cross his fingers and hope that Hadley hadn't seen his timeline.

A new notification popped up. Derrick scrolled to the top of his profile. Someone had tagged him in a picture. The thumbnail showed nothing but a jumbled blur. Reluctantly, Derrick clicked the link. The image filled the screen.

It showed a big black cat, baring a mouthful of sharp, stained teeth. Photoshopped clumsily in front of it was a fat kid with Derrick's head pasted onto its shoulders, supposedly running away from the animal. Across the bottom of the picture a caption read: THE PANTHER STALKS NATURE'S LARGEST PREY.

He'd been tagged along with his whole form group at school. So right now *everyone* would be clicking their notifications. Great.

Derrick adjusted the screen to reduce the sun's glare. The image didn't make any sense.

Then he remembered the scuffling in the alley last night. The rattle of the chain-link fence. The black fur caught on the metal.

School had only just started for the day, but people had been posting things to each other all morning from their phones. One article appeared several times over. It was a link to the local newspaper's website. No one at school read the local paper.

The headline read: POLICE HUNT BIG CAT IN SOUTH LONDON.

Derrick skimmed excitedly through the story. From the very first paragraph he realised that he knew it all already. An old lady who lived on the road over the other side of the allotments had spotted a creature prowling her garden. The police took it seriously enough to dispatch a chopper.

Derrick shivered. He'd *been* there.

There was a stock picture of a panther. Startling green eyes were scrunched up as it snarled with enormous jaws. It had a long body thick with black fur and muscle. Five times the size of the neighbourhood foxes.

Halfway down the page was a picture he'd seen before. A blurry photo of a garden wall, and what looked like hind legs and a long black tail disappearing over the other side. Three months ago the sighting had been buried deep in the newspaper. Nobody had paid much attention. But Derrick had. He remembered staring at it while he was stuck in the hospital waiting room.

The panther had first appeared on the night of Charlotte's incident, and in the three months since then everything had spun out of his control – his weight, his friendship with Tamoor – and it was only getting worse. Try as he might, he couldn't make it stop. The panther roamed free while he was trapped in this nightmare.

He replayed the previous night in his mind. The helicopter must have spotted him in the alley. In the darkness they might have confused him for the panther. He had obviously been worth checking out, anyway. What nobody had noticed was: it had been *right there*, stuck in the fence, just moments before.

There was nothing else it could have been.

Something on the screen caught his eye. An update

from three days ago: *Tamoor Hussein and Hadley Childs became friends.*

He fumbled with the touchpad and clicked through to Hadley's profile. The familiar profile photo greeted him: her red hair flung across her eyes, the studs in her lip blazing with the camera flash. But now wasn't the time to linger like he usually would.

The post from Tamoor glared out at him from the top of her timeline. A single word: *Hey.*

She hadn't replied. Not publicly, anyway. Derrick would have seen it.

They shouldn't know each other. He struggled to breathe. Hot panic flushed through his chest. The thought of all the things he'd told Tamoor about her, about his feelings for her, terrified him.

Hadley's profile picture had obviously been taken at some party. There had been other friends in the photo but she'd chopped them out. A disembodied elbow floated over her head.

Derrick's family had known Hadley's family for as long as he'd been alive. They lived just at the end of his road and a little way up the hill that trailed onto the high street. And as long as Derrick could remember he'd loved Hadley. It didn't matter that she was older than him, and several miles out of his league. Love is blind. He'd probably have had a better shot if she was, too.

In all the confusion of the last few months there was only one thing that Derrick had stayed sure of: Hadley was his only chance to be happy. If he could break free of this darkness and be with her, things would be ok again. He needed that more than anything.

'Is that who you were thinking about in the changing room yesterday?'

Derrick slammed the laptop shut. He turned around to find Charlotte standing in his doorway. A faded grey T-shirt hung from one of her shoulders. Sleep had frizzed out her long hair. It had been a while since she'd bothered with the makeup she used to hide the rash of spots around her throat.

'Get out of my room,' he said. Though he couldn't protest too hard. It *had* been Hadley he'd thought about in the changing room the day before.

'You should shut the door if you're going to do that kind of thing.'

His belly folded in front of him as he scooted to sit on the edge of his bed. One hand tugged his T-shirt loose before it could get caught in his flesh.

There was always a strange tension between them now. A fragility in the air that neither of them wanted to break. They had lived together their entire lives, and in the space of three months they had practically become strangers. Just the sight of her made him angry.

It wasn't worth getting into an argument. Not without Mum there to pick up the pieces. He just wanted her to leave him alone.

Then his eyes caught on her skinny arms, folded across her chest. The skin was criss-crossed with faint cutting scars, almost like they'd been drawn on. He could never understand why she used to cut herself. He'd Googled it once, but the answers didn't make any sense to him.

The whole thing didn't make any sense to him. *Depression*. She didn't have anything to be depressed *about*. It was her making everyone else's life miserable.

'It's weird to keep looking at her Facebook, you know.'

Charlotte and Hadley had been friends pretty much for ever, in the way that girls tend to conduct their friendships. They'd erupt into arguments every few weeks, only to forgive each other like it was nothing after a few days. As far as he knew, Hadley was the only one of Charlotte's friends who knew about the incident. It wasn't as if it could have stayed hidden from her. Their families were too close.

Silence fell between them. It would have been the perfect moment for her to leave. Instead she leaned her bony shoulder against the doorframe and stared past him out of the window. Derrick found himself staring at the crop of stubble on her legs.

The problem was that if they didn't argue, neither of them knew what to say to each other any more.

The anger clipped his words. But there was something else too. Whenever she was around, clammy fear settled on his skin. It didn't make sense, but he thought it felt a lot like guilt. A strange sensation that he had let her down somehow.

Charlotte broke the silence. 'Did you see about the panther?'

The Beast. The words echoed inside his head like a low growl before he could stop them. It sounded right. 'Yeah, I just read about it.'

Excitement tingled across his skin. For a second he

wanted to tell her about last night. How he'd almost seen it with his own two eyes, just a few feet away from him in the darkness. The thought of her asking why he'd been out prowling the alley in the first place kept him quiet. That was the last thing he wanted her to know.

Even though it's her fault you were there.

Charlotte leaned on the doorframe for just a moment longer. Her eyes grew distant, as if she were imagining it: the Beast as it roamed the streets around their house. Absolutely free, escaped from wherever it had been penned up. Charlotte's face looked almost hopeful. It was the first time in weeks he'd seen her interested in anything that wasn't exam revision or crying.

As soon as she left the room, Derrick opened his laptop and searched *How catch . . .* Google remembered, and auto-completed the search.

How catch panther?

Chapter Three

Traffic passed at a crawl along the main road in the congestion of the school run. Exhaust fumes hung heavy in the afternoon heat. Such slow progress gave passengers plenty of time to spot Derrick as he leaned back against the low wooden front fence of the house. Most of them ignored him, which is exactly what he wanted. But every now and then someone from his school would pass by, getting a lift home with a parent. Their eyes would light up when they saw him, but their choice of hand gestures made it quite clear that they weren't exactly happy to see him in the traditional sense.

After twenty minutes of waiting a bus edged past, packed with guys from school. They beat on the windows so hard it sounded like the glass would break. It made the driver stop to shout at them, which just gave them more time to mouth *WANKER* at him. When the bus eventually crawled away it made Derrick feel like he was the only attraction on a really disappointing theme park ride.

He pretended to play on his phone. His face grew

hot. Tamoor should be home by now. He'd never liked to hang around once school was finished. In fact, they'd worked out a route that got them to the bus stop early, allowing them to take the journey before it got too crowded. Maybe Tamoor had retired that routine along with their friendship. Derrick didn't know – he'd started getting a different bus that took twenty minutes longer, just to avoid being hassled by anyone.

It took less than a week for Tamoor to cut Derrick out of his life. First there was the argument at their usual hangout, the derelict warehouse just over the fence on the far side of the allotments. The bus stop was the first warning sign that the damage might be permanent. Every morning they'd met there, without fail. But at the beginning of the week Tamoor didn't show. Derrick had let the usual bus go by and sent a text to see if he was off sick. There was no reply.

When Derrick walked into form – ten minutes late – and found Tamoor already there, he didn't give it much thought. Like always he sat right next to him. When he'd asked what had happened, Tamoor mumbled something about getting a lift with somebody else.

Any talk between them for the rest of the day had gone in one direction only. Tamoor would only answer if he absolutely had to, and even then with just a single word or shrug. At lunchtime he took the last seat at a table full of meatheads, forcing Derrick to sit elsewhere. That was when he'd become aware that something was seriously wrong.

That had been three months ago. Ten days after Charlotte's incident. They'd spent those ten days traipsing around and around the allotments, trying to catch a glimpse of the panther. He couldn't forget that picture in the newspaper. The panther had escaped on the same day that his whole family had become trapped. It couldn't have just been a coincidence.

It had made him feel *jealous*.

In the end Tamoor lost his temper. That was when Derrick told him everything that had happened at home.

That's how Tamoor knew it was Charlotte's fault. There was no other reason he suddenly decided to start hanging around with the school meatheads they'd always tried to avoid. It was because of Charlotte. There was no other explanation.

Sweat leaked out of his forehead in fat beads. The sun felt hot enough to crack open his skin. Now that he was carrying all that extra weight he definitely felt the heat more. It was only a ten-minute walk to Tamoor's house, but even that was enough to get him out of breath. Derrick glanced up and down the main road for any sign of Tamoor. The traffic was moving more smoothly now. The cars seemed to blur into glints and shimmers of sunlight.

The friendship hadn't ended with a punch in the mouth. Maybe he should be grateful for that, but it might have been easier to understand than simply being phased out, as if he'd somehow ceased to exist. It felt like Charlotte's depression had cut him off from, cut him out of, real life, and sealed him away inside a poor impression of it.

After yesterday's prank, Derrick knew that he

shouldn't be at Tamoor's house. But there was no one else he could go to for help. He didn't really have any other friends. This was something that he had to do. And Tamoor was the only friend he'd ever had.

'Derrick.'

His heart jolted, and he spun around to find Tamoor behind him. One hand was already resting on the chipped paint of his front gate, as if he were thinking about making a run for the door. Derrick wouldn't exactly be fast enough to catch him. You could tell it was Friday by Tamoor's uniform: shirt untucked, collar open, a sliver of tie like a striped tongue flopping out of his pocket. His trousers were pitched precisely, precariously, halfway down his arse. That was a look Derrick had always hated. Tamoor only started doing it recently.

'You here to stab me or something?'

Derrick held up his empty hands like it was a serious allegation. 'It's nothing to do with yesterday.'

Tamoor couldn't have got the usual bus. Derrick had watched the main road the whole time. So if Tamoor had got a different bus home, he must have come from the high street. That would bring him down the hill and past Derrick's house. It was a route that would take at least twenty minutes longer than if he got their usual bus.

Tamoor ran a hand through his slickly gelled black hair, the only part of him that still looked neat and tidy. 'What, then?'

Derrick took a self-conscious step closer. One hand automatically tugged on the hem of his T-shirt. He couldn't remember when that habit had started. It never used to be so awkward between them.

Derrick was going to put that right. 'I need your help with something.'

Tamoor looked him up and down, as if he were sizing up an old enemy. Then he turned to scan the street. A group of kids were hanging around outside the Costcutter a little further on, but otherwise there was no one that might see him talking to the fat kid from school.

'It better not be what I think it is.'

'The news that's been going round today,' said Derrick. 'About the panther?'

As he'd searched online it had soon become clear that it wasn't just the local paper that had picked up the story. All the sites for the major papers featured it. It was even on the local TV news, the reporter standing right outside the allotment fence. At the back of the shot you could see the entrance to the alley that led to Derrick's back gate.

Seeing the panther on TV made Derrick feel weirdly protective. *He* had almost seen the panther. It had come to *him*. And now all these vultures were leaping in to get a piece. Derrick had to make sure he got there first.

Tamoor groaned and leaned against the gate. 'I *knew* that was going to set you off again.'

Derrick ignored that. 'I want to find it.'

A lorry thundered by on the road. Its cargo rattled and thumped over the uneven tarmac.

'That didn't really go so well last time, did it?

'It's real!' said Derrick. 'The police were out and everything.'

'Yeah, and they couldn't find it even with a helicopter.'

Derrick picked at a splinter of wood that hung from the fence. 'It's important for me to find it. And I've got no one else who can help me.'

The edge of Tamoor's lip curled into something resembling a sneer. Whenever Derrick tried to speak to him in front of the meatheads, that was the face Tamoor would pull. But now it seemed half-hearted. Almost sad. He flicked his eyes away, as if he didn't like what he was about to say.

'I'm sorry, but I ain't doing all that again. It made you crazy.'

It wasn't so long ago that Derrick wouldn't have needed to ask, it would have gone without saying. Now his former best friend wouldn't even look at him.

'Fine,' said Derrick, and pushed past him to head back home.

'Hang on.'

Derrick stopped at the edge of the road and turned around on the spot. Tamoor glanced back at his house, and then crossed his arms and hunched his shoulders. Even now he still wouldn't meet Derrick's eye.

'Is everything all right?' he half mumbled into his shirt. 'With your sister and that?'

The day he had told Tamoor about it the dark interior of the warehouse was filled with flying ants, swarming around the corrugated metal walls like a plague. So they'd sat together out front on the cracked concrete forecourt, leaning back against the rusted air-conditioning units. In the sun the whole place still smelled like smoke and petrol.

It had been the first time Derrick had spoken to anyone about it.

It was the real end of their friendship.

That was the moment that he was exiled, finally and utterly, from the rest of the world.

Derrick could never forget Tamoor's reaction. It had put a sudden end to their argument. Tamoor had silently picked at the weeds that grew through the cracks in the concrete. Then, just like now, he'd refused to meet his eye.

Derrick hadn't been back to the warehouse since.

'I'll catch the bloody panther without your help!' he shouted, storming across the road.

Tamoor shouted after him. 'Why d'you care so much?'

Derrick shoved his hands deep into his pockets and didn't look back. It was a question that he didn't know how to answer.

Chapter Four

When Charlotte really kicked off she cried like nails were being hammered into her tongue. A single, piercing wail would be followed by a few seconds of silence. It was just enough time for whatever was causing her such pain to land another blow. The next long wail would be harsher, almost a guttural scream.

The noise sluiced down the stairs and flooded the hallway, even though her bedroom door was closed. Derrick flinched and finished tying his shoelaces. It had been a while since the last big cry. For the last few weeks she'd been mostly silent and withdrawn. Which meant that when something set her off the crying would be cataclysmic. It was as if all the pain she'd managed to keep hidden for so long was puking itself out all at once.

It had happened during dinner.

'Next week is your last exam,' said Mum.

Charlotte cut carelessly into her burger with the edge of a spoon. 'I know.'

'I haven't seen you doing much work.'

The spoon clattered against the plate. Charlotte

glared at her roughly dissected dinner and huffed out a breath. That was the first sign. Derrick had fought the urge to run. Burger be damned.

Mum noticed, but went on anyway. 'It takes a lot of work to get to university.'

'Like anyone in this family would know.'

Silence. Another long breath. And *wham!* She exploded like a can of beans in a microwave. If there was a world record for fleeing up the stairs in tears, Charlotte would hold it.

This was how things had been – long weeks of silence followed by a detonation that shook the entire house. It was happening again now, just like before the incident. The thought of it made him shiver. Derrick blinked it away.

The only way he knew to deal with it was to get out of the house. The crying seemed to make the air grow heavy, like the hour before a storm. He couldn't stand it. If he stayed inside he could do nothing but silently will her to shut up. It made him feel guilt that was almost unbearable. He should be able to do something. He should be able to do more than hate her for it.

Getting out of the house, trying to escape the darkness that threatened to choke him inside its walls, let him pretend that it was possible to escape it all. And that night, finally, he had another reason for leaving.

'I'm going for a run!' he shouted up the stairs. No answer. They probably wouldn't even notice that he was gone.

He patted the bulge in his jogging bottoms pocket to

check that the cat food tin was secure. Then he slammed the front door shut behind him.

Even though he had waited until it was dark it was still warm enough to be comfortable in his T-shirt (XXL, with some faded foreign writing on the front). The heavy tin tugged at his jogging bottoms as he strode along the pavement. He had to hold them up by the waist.

The Internet wasn't terribly helpful on how to hunt panthers. Well, not unless it involved blasting their heads off with a rifle. As he made his way along the road Derrick wondered how many panthers he'd need to kill to make a fur coat big enough to fit him. It would probably endanger the species.

He'd looked at hundreds of different pictures of the animal online. They were completely black, which wouldn't exactly make it easy to spot. Their most striking feature was a pair of round, green eyes that reflected light like blazing mirrors.

Why do you care so much? Tamoor's question echoed in his head. The answer still hadn't come to him. It just felt important that he find it. Last time he had given up after ten days. Since then things had only got worse. While the Beast was free, his family never would be. It was the only thing he had left that made sense.

This time he wouldn't give up. The way things were going, he probably didn't have much time.

The Beast. The name came to him out of nowhere. Somehow it felt right. He said it aloud, the words rumbling out of him like a growl. The shape of his lips as he spoke made him tremble.

The track to the allotments was just before the end of his road. It cut directly through the houses on his side of the street. Whenever Derrick told Mum that he was going for a run, he'd usually carry on to the end of the road and head downhill to get an ice cream or something at Tesco. It wasn't exactly as if she'd notice. Charlotte took up all of her attention these days.

If he turned uphill at the end of the road instead, he could walk past Hadley's house. It wouldn't be the first time. Sometimes he just walked past in the hope that he might catch a glimpse of her. So far it had never happened.

Instead he turned into the allotment track, into the darkness between the houses. It was wide enough for a car. A ridge of grass grew up between a pair of dirt tyre tracks.

Derrick stopped at the gate, where the news reporter had stood. There was just enough light from the back windows of the nearby houses to make out the cigarette butts scattered in the dirt. Derrick grabbed the rusty padlock on the gate. Only official plot owners held a key. To his right was the entrance to the alley. If he followed it down to his own back gate he could find the ragged hole in the chain-link. But he might get stuck halfway through. They wouldn't find him until the morning, his legs chewed off by the Beast. That was pretty much the last thing he needed.

Instead he sucked in a breath, tugged his T-shirt down, and wedged a foot into the metal gate.

It clattered gently. The gate wasn't much taller than him, but his legs still burned ferociously as he heaved himself up to straddle it. Then it was just a case of shifting his weight and swinging his other leg over.

The impact of landing jarred into his hips. Before he could even notice it the weight of the cat food tugged at his jogging bottoms and pulled them down around his ankles. For just a second the warm night air washed through the holes in his pants.

'Bugger!'

Quickly he yanked them back up and held them at the waist with one hand while he fished the tin out with the other. Access to the allotments was forbidden to the public. If someone spotted him wandering about in the dark with his trousers down they'd call the police. That would be the icing on the cake after what had happened at school. They'd start calling him a sex offender.

He paused to allow himself a few breaths. There wasn't much chance of anyone spotting him. That's what he told himself to try and stay calm. The allotments didn't have lighting of their own. Just what reached in from the nearby houses. It was enough for him to make out the grassy paths that squeezed between vegetable patches. A clump of sheds sat just ahead of him, surrounded by mismatched garden furniture.

One of these patches belonged to Hadley's dad. Derrick remembered her telling him about it. Her dad was a butcher, and had become a bit obsessed with organic food. That meant that going over there for dinner was rarely a delicious experience.

Derrick skirted around the sheds, past a vegetable patch built tall with bean poles and another full of dark lumps that might have been cabbages or something. Vegetables weren't exactly Derrick's strong point. The musty smell of churned earth clung to his nostrils. When he got towards the back of the allotments he ducked under the kiddie swing set and stopped underneath the big oak.

The back of the allotments seemed to be utilised as some kind of dumping ground. The fence was blocked off by overgrowth, thick bushes tangled with nettles. A couple of smaller trees grew in the shadow of the oak. A mound of dead branches rose out of the weeds, and here and there was discarded gardening equipment, a couple of old fencing panels, an abandoned wooden crate. Derrick had no doubt about it: this would be the best place for the Beast to hide out.

He lifted his head to listen. There was no sign of any helicopter now. Music drifted over from a nearby house, and there was the usual hum of distant traffic. The Internet had told him that panthers have sensitive hearing. Maybe the music would be enough to mask Derrick's breathing.

Excitement flickered in his chest.

The allotments stretched the entire length of his street, and were easily as wide as several houses put together. The top of the derelict warehouse was just visible at the far end beyond the perimeter fence. Almost directly opposite the tree he could make out his own house, the bathroom window a perfect square of yellow light.

Derrick felt absolutely calm. The allotments felt like some kind of nature reserve, protected from the corrosion of depression. He took a deep breath. It felt easier to fill his lungs here.

He lifted the cat food tin to catch the light and dug his nails under the ring-pull. It opened with a metallic *crack*. The smell slapped him in the face, like gravy that had been left out in the sun for a week.

That's when he realised that he'd forgotten to bring a dish or anything. With the tin at arm's length he looked around for something that would do the job. He *could* just dump it on the ground. He didn't know if a panther would be fussy about that. There was a patch of grass just ahead of him that wasn't concealed by the shadow of the tree. That would make it easier for him to keep watch.

Derrick upturned the tin. The cat food didn't budge. It remained stubbornly inside even when he shook it and whacked it with the flat of his hand. Some kind of juice splashed over his jogging bottoms.

'Oh, come on, seriously?'

He choked back a retch. This was probably what the dustbin cookies had been soaked with. The thought made him cringe, and he bashed the tin hard against the ground. The cat food still refused to evacuate. Derrick groaned, loudly, knowing what he had to do.

'You'd better appreciate this, Beasty.'

His fingers sunk down into the cat food. It sucked and spluttered like viscous mud. He held his breath and scooped out a wet handful. It glooped onto the grass. Its coldness made him shudder. Half the gunk stuck to his fingers, forcing him to shake it loose. Slime sprayed into his face. He doubled over, spitting and coughing, but delved his hand in again before he lost his nerve. The second handful slopped on top of the first to form a glistening brown mound in the grass.

Derrick launched the rest of the tin as hard as he could into the bushes. It landed somewhere in the darkness with a soft *clank*. It took several long minutes of dragging his hand through the grass before he was reasonably satisfied that it was clean.

The Internet had said that the best way to lure a panther was 'live bait'. This would just have to do.

Derrick retreated behind the thick trunk of the oak tree. He'd checked before leaving the house that his phone had enough charge to shoot a video. Now he leaned against the rough tree bark, phone poised and ready to record as soon as the Beast revealed itself. As he stared at the brown lump of cat food, Derrick wondered what he would do with the video of the Beast. It would make sense to put it on YouTube. That way TV and the newspapers would see it, and they'd know that he got there first. It would be official. It was *his* catch.

It might just be enough for him to know for sure that the panther was there. A big part of him felt that he just wanted to keep the video to himself. Somehow it would feel wrong to expose it to the world like that.

He had to get the footage first. The bait didn't exactly look appetising, but his cat at home ate it all the time, so it should be good enough for a panther.

The music nearby suddenly went quiet. A dog barked in protest from one of the nearby gardens.

Derrick watched on his phone as twenty minutes ticked by. After a while even the dog got bored and decided to shut up. Nothing stirred in the allotments. Maybe the Beast could smell him.

Maybe YOU'RE the live bait.

Derrick shivered. Maybe it was time to go home, anyway. The jogging story was tenuous enough without him being gone for ages. Although they probably wouldn't even have noticed yet that he was gone. When Charlotte started crying like that it would go on for hours, until she was too exhausted to keep it up. The silence that followed always felt eerie. Like an unexplained absence.

The weeds rustled behind him. Derrick froze.

A hunter can recognise a trap.

The sound came from the bushes. It was a low growl that seemed like little more than a breath of wind. But Derrick felt it rumble inside his chest. He tried to make his body turn but it refused. Suddenly he felt just like the cat food trapped inside the tin. Now more than ever he didn't want to be eaten alive.

Dead twigs and dirt crackled softly, the sound of something padding cautiously through the undergrowth.

Goose pimples prickled across his skin. His hand on the phone grew clammy with sweat. The rustling was gentle but growing louder. Closer. Derrick let out a shaky breath and gripped his phone hard.

In one quick movement he spun around and swiped the screen to life. In its pale white light a black shape darted clear of the bushes, just a few metres in front of him. It disappeared into the darkness before Derrick could even hope to see it.

Without thinking he pushed himself away from the tree and launched after it, setting his phone recording and carrying it clumsily in front of him.

The night hid the creature completely. There was only the noise of thrashing leaves ahead of him. Derrick saw the plants ripple in the closest vegetable patch. He stomped after it and kicked the plants out of his way, stumbling on the uneven soil. By the time he reached the other side his lungs were burning.

He rushed blindly forward into the next patch. Something caught his foot and he tumbled over and landed hard in the soil. The phone skittered out of his hand. Derrick forced himself up, trampling vegetables under his feet.

A stitch bit into his side. Sweat dripped into his eyes. When he stumbled out on the other side of the patch he paused to listen. There was nothing but his hard, heaving breaths. Hurriedly he scanned the surrounding patches, peered underneath a nearby wheelbarrow, through the chain-link fence. No sign of anything moving at all.

It was the Beast. Even though he didn't see it, Derrick could *feel* it. It had spoken to him. It wanted him to know that it was there. This was closer than he had ever come before.

He walked slowly, his eyes wide, back to the oak tree. He was panting so hard still that he startled a fox who had come to investigate the cat food.

It was only when he turned for the gate that he

remembered his phone. He looked back at the patches and tried to remember where he had fallen but in the darkness they all looked the same.

'Bugger.'

He was still short of breath when he arrived at his front door. Fat droplets of sweat trickled down his face.

Mum was standing in the hall. That meant that Charlotte must have calmed down enough to be left alone. Or she'd started screaming and throwing things until Mum had to escape for her own safety.

Mum studied the dirt and sweat that covered him, a glass of something pungently alcoholic poised halfway to her lips.

'Looks like you had a good jog.'

Derrick shrugged. He felt exhausted – and not just because running didn't exactly agree with him. The short chase across the allotments had been exhilarating, actually; his heart was still pounding.

For the first time in months – in the allotments, with the Beast so close – he had felt truly free. Now that he was back inside the house the air seemed rigid and stifling. It hurt his lungs to breathe. A sense of quiet desperation closed around him, sealing him off from the outside world. The house was like a fish bowl, black oil spreading slowly through the water.

He felt how that voice had vibrated inside his chest.

The house was the trap. That's what the Beast had meant. He recognised it now.

Instead of trying to explain any of this to Mum, he just shrugged again and stomped upstairs to his room.

Chapter Five

'I'm not even sure where you'd buy night vision goggles in Croydon, anyway.'

Derrick had decided that it would take a little more than a tin of cat food to catch the Beast. But he realised that he hadn't really thought through some of the finer details of his latest plan. Lounging back on his dad's sofa, he scratched a pen across his shopping list.

~~Night vision goggles.~~

'How about you tell me what you need these things for and maybe I'll think about it,' said Dad.

Derrick tried to think how he could tell the truth without sounding completely crazy. *Sure, Dad, I'm hunting a wild panther that lives at the bottom of the garden.* Yeah, right.

Still, it had been in the papers so much that Dad had probably read about it already. The problem last time was that Derrick hadn't taken it seriously enough. The main issue now was that special equipment was expensive, and he had approximately no money whatsoever. Derrick could usually convince Dad to buy him things. Probably a result of whatever guilt was left over from the divorce. But this might have been pushing it too far.

He ran his eyes down his list: *big metal cage, lots of rope, ~~night vision goggles~~, tranquilliser darts.* Now that he looked again, it read more like the list of a convicted kidnapper. Or worse. He screwed it up into a ball before Dad could get a look.

'Never mind.'

Dad shrugged and returned to folding his laundry away into the airing cupboard. They rarely did much on these visits. Derrick had considered staying home to keep an eye on the allotments. That morning he'd watched through the bathroom window as a couple of policemen walked between the vegetable patches. They spent half an hour wandering to the far end, and then back again. Derrick had held his breath, waiting for them to find his phone. But they seemed to leave without finding anything at all.

Dad's flat was on the top floor of a rundown council block. Nicer on the inside, but not by much. The walls were stained with damp, so every room had the slightly tangy smell of seaweed. The floors were bare wood, meaning footsteps thudded around the whole flat. The neighbours below had to just hate his visits.

It had been around a year since Dad moved here. A year since the daily shouting matches between his parents had ended in the inevitable. It wasn't exactly a surprise when Dad announced that he was moving out. In fact, Derrick had been surprised at how little it had bothered him. He'd thought it would make everyone happier. Especially Charlotte. It was while the

44

arguing raged on that Derrick had first noticed something was wrong with his sister. She'd started spending every night shut in her room. The sound of her crying would drift through the door for hours. When the frosty silence between his parents thawed into screaming, Charlotte's sobs would join in to form a symphony of discord.

As Derrick waited it out in his room, he'd assumed that the two were linked. Maybe Charlotte had just been taking the impending divorce badly.

Then Dad left. And the crying didn't stop. The atmosphere in the house only seemed to get worse. Derrick was the only man left, and it felt like his duty to fix it. So far he wasn't doing a very good job.

The new flat was only a short drive away. A bus stopped pretty much right outside. Almost immediately after the split Derrick had started spending as much time there as possible. It wasn't because he particularly missed his dad. He was just glad to get away from home. It had felt like he was running away. But for a while it had been the only place where the tension in his stomach would ease off.

It had only lasted for a couple of months. Every time Dad asked how things were going, or sighed and rubbed his eyes, a little darkness crept in. He could practically see it seeping through the floorboards. Derrick had thought that he could escape here.

It wouldn't be as easy as that.

Dad balanced the last of the washing inside the cupboard and slammed the door shut before it could topple back out. Then he padded across the wooden floor and

45

threw himself back into the armchair opposite Derrick. The movement was too exaggerated to be genuinely casual. That meant something awkward was coming.

'How's your sister doing?'

Derrick squirmed in his seat. After a while Charlotte had started to join him on these visits. That was when it had stopped being a sanctuary. Even then they never did much, but she seemed to enjoy the slight change of scenery. She almost seemed relaxed, although by that point it was getting hard to tell.

The crying became sort of a game. Derrick would try and work out what ridiculous thing would make her cry next. Her friends doing something together at school without her, even though she'd long stopped going. Mum complaining about how much food was left on her plate, even though she'd pretty much stopped eating. Most of the time there didn't seem to be any real reason for it at all. That was what had annoyed Derrick the most.

One night she began to scream as if someone were trying to murder her. She smashed everything in her room against the walls. One of the neighbours called the police. It had been Derrick who'd answered the door. The sight of the policemen standing there had made his heart leap into his mouth. He'd only been able to swallow it again when he saw that everything was ok. Nobody was hurt or anything. Not on the outside, anyway.

A week later the doctor diagnosed her with depression. And that's when things really started to go wrong: the crying stopped almost completely.

Derrick managed to shrug. 'She's ok, I suppose. You know.'

There was so much more that he could say. But he never did. No one really wanted to talk about Charlotte. It always felt too uncomfortable. Derrick found it too difficult to swallow his anger. To reconcile it with the underlying guilt.

Everything had changed after the incident. Dad and Charlotte began to argue every time she visited.

About a month later they had such a big blow-out that they hadn't spoken since. Derrick hadn't been there. No one had told him what it was about. All he knew was that now he visited on his own. Dad wouldn't even go inside the house when he arrived to pick him up or drop him off.

It was just another example of how she was tearing the family apart. How her depression had closed them off from the rest of the world.

A thought dropped suddenly into his brain. *It's another reason why you need to find the Beast.*

Dad nodded, his eyes growing distant. That seemed to happen whenever they talked about Charlotte. 'Why don't you check the junk cupboard for anything useful?'

Derrick raised an eyebrow as he heaved himself up, tugged at his T-shirt, and dragged his feet over to the cupboard door at the end of the sitting room. The sight that greeted him wasn't exactly encouraging. Old football magazines spilled out from torn cardboard boxes, shelves up to the ceiling were loaded with old electronics and VHS tapes, and a single mattress still wrapped in plastic was pushed to the back. A worn-out suit hung from a nail in the wall. It was hardly the Bat Cave. The chances of finding anything useful were slim. But he'd take any excuse to escape further conversation about his sister.

'Keep an eye out for anything your sister might want for uni,' shouted Dad. 'I'd like to help if I can.'

The last thing she'd want for her new life was any of this old junk. Derrick started by lifting a box of cassette tapes from the top of the stack. The box underneath it held nothing but a knotted snarl of electrical cables. Not really the kind of rope he was after. Next he lifted a threadbare sheet to uncover a crate loaded with old stationery, pens and elastic bands, a stapler and some stiff paint brushes. Half submerged was a black cylinder with what looked like a glass lens. Derrick pulled it clear and saw that it was a pair of binoculars.

They were matt black, dirty, probably way older than he was. But the plastic felt tough. He lifted them to his eyes and peered through. The book spines leaped towards him, their names and authors almost pin-sharp. They weren't exactly the night vision goggles he wanted, but with a bit of a polish they could prove useful.

He kept searching. The bottom of the next box collapsed when he lifted it, depositing folders and papers across the floor. Derrick abandoned it and kept riffling through unlabelled videos, a box full of outdated music magazines, a broken ironing board, a folding chair. He hated the idea that life was this boring. If someone rooted through his stuff in fifty years' time, would it all be as dull as this?

You could hide a live grenade in your possessions. He was still contemplating the idea when he stumbled across a set of handcuffs at the top of a rusted toolbox. They were heavier than he expected. The coldness of the metal made it clear they were the real thing. The cuffs were open, and Derrick searched the rest of the toolbox unsuccessfully for the key.

'Dad?' he shouted back over his shoulder.

Derrick tugged his T-shirt down, scooped up the binoculars, and backed out of the junk cupboard without bothering to tidy up. Moving the boxes had made him slightly out of breath. A film of sweat prickled on his forehead.

Dad heaved himself out of the armchair. 'Find anything?'

Derrick held up the handcuffs. 'Why do you have these?'

Dad tried to bite back a smile. 'They belonged to your mother.'

'Oh gross!' Derrick dropped the cuffs as if they were poisonous. They landed on his foot with a heavy *thud*. 'Ow!'

'You asked.' Dad retrieved the cuffs and let the smile break across his face. 'Want them?'

Derrick tried to ignore the throbbing in his foot. They *could* come in handy. Though he wasn't sure how just yet. You probably couldn't handcuff a panther.

He snatched them back. 'I'm washing them first.'

After dinner Dad drove him home. They pulled up under the streetlight outside Derrick's house. Usually he would just say a quick goodbye and head inside. But as his fingers gripped the door handle he felt like he had a duty to do more. If Dad wasn't going to try and fix it, Derrick would do it for him.

He tried to keep his voice casual. 'Come inside, if you want.'

'That's probably not a good idea.'

'Come on, you can't argue forever.'

Dad wrung the steering wheel between his hands and let out a long breath. It was as if just the idea of going inside the house exhausted him. 'It'll just upset your sister.'

Derrick gritted his teeth and squeezed the door handle. The plastic creaked. It was impossible *not* to upset her. They all spent their entire lives tiptoeing around her, too scared of saying anything that might set her off. It wasn't fair that she was allowed to wreck their lives. To keep them all trapped like snails inside a jar.

'Look, I don't know what I'm supposed to do, ok?' said Dad. 'Just tell her I said good luck for her exam.'

'What did you argue about?' said Derrick quickly. It was the first time he'd asked about it.

Dad turned his eyes to look through the windscreen, pausing as if to work out exactly the right words. It was something he never quite managed with Charlotte. Somehow whatever came out of his mouth seemed to piss her off.

'Your sister blames me for her depression.'

Derrick turned to face him. 'Because of the divorce? Bullshit.'

'Language,' said Dad. He breathed out a long sigh. 'I

50

know I left at a bad time. I'm not proud of that. But there's something I should have told you a lot sooner. I have the same problem that she does.'

Derrick stared. It took him a few seconds to work out what he meant. 'You mean depression? You're like her?'

Dad nodded guiltily. In response Derrick shook his head. The information wouldn't sink in. It didn't make any sense at all. Dad didn't behave anything like Charlotte. There was no screaming or crying. He could be a bit grumpy sometimes. And he used to shout at Mum. But that was just Dad. He was too *normal* to have depression.

Dad seemed to guess what he was thinking. 'You have to understand that it's not the same for everyone. I've lived with it a lot longer than she has. I can't tell you that it gets better. It's never easy. But I've learned to cope with it, I think. Your sister is angry that I didn't tell her about it until . . . after. She thinks I should have done more to help her. I'm not sure that she's wrong.'

Derrick was suddenly furious. It took him a moment to speak. Nobody told *him* any of this. Charlotte's depression was such a big deal, but Dad had managed to keep his hidden for all this time.

'It still doesn't explain why she blames you.'

Self-consciously Dad shifted to put a hand on his shoulder. 'It can be genetic. She might have inherited it from me.'

Derrick shook his head. No words could make it as far as his lips.

51

'Sometimes the only way to cope is to find someone to blame,' said Dad. 'It makes it easier to understand.'

For just a second Derrick felt like he was going to cry. A black bubble seemed to expand from the house, trapping them both inside it. Soon it would grow so big that there would be nowhere to escape from it. The only place that was safe now was the allotments.

He bit back the tears and shoved Dad's hand off his shoulder, then pushed open the car door.

'It's not that I didn't want to help –'

Derrick slammed the door shut before he could hear the rest of the sentence. He stamped across the pavement and ran for the house.

Chapter Six

The alley showed no sign of what had happened a couple of nights ago. The dustbins had been emptied, but the warm, sticky smell of ripened rubbish still remained. Derrick leaned down to peer through the hole in the fence. No sign of black fur.

The allotments seemed as tranquil as always. An overcast sky made it darker than usual. Through the sheds and beanpoles he could barely see to the back. Only the wavering branches of the oak tree stood out against the sky. A car alarm spiralled in the distance.

Anger had threatened to overcome him when he ran from the car. Now he began to relax. It was the allotments. Somehow they drained his anger. They were the only place that he felt free. The Beast was on the loose here, free of the trap, free of the depression that had sealed away everywhere else in his life.

The wooden fence creaked as he leaned back against it. He kicked at a newspaper by his feet. Dad had depression too. The revelation wouldn't sink in even now that his anger had faded. He'd never seen Dad crying or screaming or smashing things against the wall. Arguments with Mum had been heated. They'd always tried to keep it quiet, as if Derrick wouldn't notice. Then suddenly the whispers would ignite into furious shouting like a struck match. Maybe it was the depression that made him behave that way. Maybe the depression was the real reason they'd split up. But Mum had done plenty of shouting too.

A father was supposed to look after their family. That's what he was always told. Now that Dad was gone, someone else had to pick up the slack.

He scooped up the newspaper and read the front-page story about the panther. All sorts of people were coming forward with accounts of seeing it. *It was on my garden shed eyeing up my pet rabbit*, said one stupid woman. *It peed all over my radishes and killed them*, said an equally stupid man.

They were all liars. The Beast was there for *him*.

It was a sign that things were only going to keep getting worse. Now Dad was like Charlotte too. Derrick was the only person left who could do something about it. The Beast's freedom felt like an insult.

He let the newspaper drop and it landed on his feet. As he glanced down at it, something else caught his eye. Their garden fence was mostly hidden behind overgrown bushes, but they were cut back around the gate enough to keep it clear. Reaching forward, he brushed his fingertips along the wood just inside the gate. A vertical mark, starting as high as his chest, had been gouged deep into the grain almost down to the ground. Wide, splintered grooves. The damage stood out in the dark like a wound.

He recognised it immediately. It looked exactly like the banisters at the bottom of the stairs where their cat liked to scratch. Derrick had read about panther behaviour during his Google searches. They were highly territorial. They'd scratch somewhere to sharpen their claws and mark their turf.

The Beast had chosen his back garden.

A harsh bark from the allotments jolted him out of his thoughts. Derrick froze, but it was only a fox. He was used to being woken up by foxes screaming at each other. Another fox answered, and the two barked back and forth from opposite ends of the allotments. (As a form of communication, he didn't think it was wildly different to Facebook.) After a moment another fox joined in, and another and another.

The air grew thick with noise, a grating cacophony that tumbled over and into itself like rocks rolling down a cliff. He had to fight the urge to cover his ears. He wanted to record it and fumbled in his pockets before remembering that his phone was lost. The noise seemed to be woven into the fabric of the darkness.

Slowly, Derrick pressed his face into the cool metal of the chain-link. His breath came in shaky, irregular flurries. It sounded like a thousand foxes now, but he couldn't see a single one.

Quiet.

The low growl cut through the middle of it all and the foxes hushed. It was a growl like a rumble of thunder, which seemed to roll in from every direction, simultaneously miles away and a breath upon his neck. It shook the air and quivered inside his stomach. He squeezed the fence so hard that the metal cut into his skin.

As the growl died away, silence settled once again over the allotments, as if nothing at all had happened.

Derrick turned and ran. He didn't stop until the kitchen door was locked behind him.

Chapter Seven

There was no way Derrick was going back to school tomorrow. It was just a case of working out which reason Mum was most likely to accept for him to stay home.

For a start, the backlash from last week's video hadn't died down. His Facebook page was full of fresh abuse. If he still had his phone, he'd probably be getting texts too. There was only one week of school left before the summer holidays. That was a potential five days solid of ridicule. Approximately five days more than he wanted.

But the embarrassment wasn't even his main reason to stay home. When he woke up on Sunday morning his stomach was churning. It was hard to breathe and his arms and legs felt heavy, like he was dragging shackles. The house made him so tense – it was getting worse – and school was the same. The only place that made him feel better, or different, was the allotments. He'd spent all of Sunday standing at Mum's bedroom window, staring out the back at those scratty plots of soil and turf, watching and remembering and trying to work out why, and what it all added up to.

Derrick walked down the stairs slowly, silently rehearsing the one argument that Mum would not be able to resist. This was not his finest hour. He shouldn't do it. The thought made guilt froth in his gut. He knew he was being manipulative. And he hated that he knew so, but would do it anyway.

Mum was in the sitting room with the cat curled up in her lap. As always, a 24-hour news channel blared at her. It seemed to be the only thing she did any more. The constant loop of bad news didn't seem to bother her. Derrick wondered if she found comfort in the consistency. Maybe it was reassuring to see that terrible things were happening to other people too.

'You've just missed that weather girl you like,' said Mum, her eyes staying on the screen.

Derrick sighed, wishing he'd never mentioned that to her, but he still felt a warm twinge of disappointment. He slumped down beside her on the sofa and rearranged his T-shirt to hide the way his belly folded like a paper fan.

'And they just mentioned that panther sighting.'

Derrick flinched. 'What did they say?'

'Nothing much. Just the local news. Police are still looking into it, or something. They were playing *Jungle Book* music in the background, so I don't think they're taking it too seriously.'

You'll show them.

He took a deep breath to prepare himself. 'Mum, I have a proposition.'

'That's what you said to the weather girl when you thought I was in the kitchen.'

'Mum.'

'Would I need to give you money?'

'Nope.'

'I'm listening.'

Derrick cleared his throat. 'You know how there's only one week left of school?'

'You mean the one week of school that you're definitely going to?'

'Yeah . . . that.'

Mum reached for the remote to mute the TV. The movement disturbed the cat, who lifted her head and blinked at him sleepily. On screen the newsreader mouthed earnest bad news at them, as if offended at being silenced.

'You've got to face it eventually,' said Mum.

'Waiting the whole summer would be better than facing it tomorrow.'

Mum sighed. 'There's a lot of things we don't talk about in this family . . .'

Derrick blinked away the memory of his conversation with Dad last night. That was something that no one had ever talked to him about.

'One of the things we don't talk about is what you were caught doing in that toilet stall. Do you want to have that conversation, Derrick?'

Heat flushed underneath his skin. For a second it felt like his skull was swelling with terrified humiliation. One hand tugged hard at the hem of his T-shirt. The conversation wasn't going quite as he'd hoped.

'My exams are already over. We don't do anything in the last week!'

'You have to go to school.'

'They'll beat me up!'

'You have to go to school.'

'They'll castrate me and wear my balls as jewellery!'

'Language. And you have to go to school.'

Derrick resorted to trying to stare her down. He fixed his eyes wide and focused them right on hers. But her eyes were immovable rounds, shot through with tired blood vessels and underscored by dark rings. It was like trying to stare down the Eye of Sauron.

It was time to fully execute the plan. Derrick swallowed hard. This was too important for him to lose his nerve now.

'If I stay home I can help Charlotte revise for her final exam on Thursday. You know she's struggling.'

Mum frowned, but she held the stare. 'How can *you* help her?'

Derrick fought off a shrug. He had to look confident, even though this conversation was making him sweat. 'I can motivate her.'

The words were met by a derisive snort.

'The stress has been making her worse. I know you've seen it. Maybe if I'm around it'll help. And I can keep an eye on her. I can make sure she doesn't try something stupid again.'

Mum made her mouth a hard, straight line. It was what she always did to keep her bottom lip from wobbling. Finally she broke, looked away to the TV across the room. It showed silent footage of women crying in the smoking ruins of a bombed-out street.

He knew that he shouldn't use Charlotte's problems to his advantage. It made him feel disgusting. Only one thought kept him rooted to the sofa. The Beast was the reason they were trapped. It had upset some kind of balance in the world. If Derrick could capture it, expose it, then he would be able to save them.

Derrick didn't know how he would do it. He just knew that it was true.

Mum turned back to him and studied his face. 'I really hope you're not just saying that.'

Derrick forced himself to shake his head.

'It's funny, isn't it?' said Mum. 'How you only seem to care about Charlotte when there's something in it for you.'

Now it was Derrick who couldn't hold her gaze. 'That's not fair.'

Mum put a hand on his knee. It was what she always did to try and show that she wasn't angry. For some reason it made him want to cry. He sniffed hard.

'What's not fair is trying to take advantage of me. I don't have the energy to fight with you, too.' She sighed to emphasise the point. 'And I've never been so scared in my life.'

Derrick looked at her. He wanted to hold her hand, put an arm around her shoulders, do something to comfort her. More than anything he wanted to crawl into her lap and let her stroke his hair, just like when he was a kid.

Mum dropped her head back against the sofa as if it

were too heavy to carry. 'I'll phone the school in the morning. But you *will* help her revise and you *will* keep an eye on her. And you have to clean the bathroom.'

Derrick nodded vigorously. It wasn't quite the victory he had anticipated. But the result was the same.

He didn't know what he should say. Eventually he said, 'Do we have the *Jungle Book* on DVD?'

Mum shook her head.

'Shame.'

As soon as Mum left for work, Derrick took over her room. With the curtains pulled back he hitched up the net curtains and placed the binoculars on the sill. Then, just for their delicious company, he positioned a plate of biscuits on the bed behind him.

There was only one person out in the allotments this early, an older woman, as round as a boulder, attacking her patch with a trowel. He raised the binoculars to his eyes. They made her arse look bigger than the moon (granted, he was hardly in a position to judge these days . . .). He shifted the view over towards the oak tree and adjusted focus. No sign of the cat food; the foxes would have had it as soon as he left.

Derrick knew that the panther wouldn't be out during the day but it didn't stop him looking. It felt like *nothing* would stop him looking. He had to work out where it was hiding. He reached for a Jammy Dodger.

Suddenly he remembered his lost phone. Maybe he could spot it from up here. He crammed the biscuit into his mouth. It was a cloudy day, the grey morning light cast evenly across the ground. The vegetable patches lay in a line from the oak tree to the chain-link. Working slowly and systematically, he ran the binoculars over each one. One was thick with deep green leaves that looked familiar, but the only thing he spotted that even slightly resembled a phone was a strangely misshapen potato.

'Bugger,' he muttered.

A *click* came from the landing, followed by the scrape of Charlotte's door as it grazed the carpet. Derrick fumbled the binoculars out of sight under Mum's bed. Then he trotted out to intercept her before she had the chance to lock herself in the bathroom.

'Why aren't you at school?' she said, rubbing her eyes.

'I'm staying home to help you revise.'

Charlotte wedged a hand against her protruding hip bone. A long T-shirt hung from her shoulders and came down almost to her knees. Derrick realised that it belonged to him. He forced himself to swallow his outrage. It would be too embarrassing to mention it.

She squinted as if even the dim light of the landing were too bright. 'You can help me by getting me a glass of water.'

Before Derrick could open his mouth she'd shoved past him and locked herself in the bathroom. The window for protest had passed him by. He *would* help her revise, he'd promised that he would. But he didn't know what he was supposed to do; drag her out of bed and slam her head down into her textbooks? The idea *was* tempting.

Her bedroom door lay open in front of him. The

curtains were drawn, and he stepped into the gloom. Her bed was one of those rollout sofa things. It was upright, as if she hadn't slept at all. Her laptop, balanced on a cushion, fizzed with tinny dubstep. A dresser held her collection of ornaments, figurines family had bought her from around the world. There used to be more, before half of them had had a run-in with the wall.

Derrick knew he shouldn't be there. If she caught him she'd probably break his nose. But there might be some clue here, something that would show him how he could make all this sadness stop.

Pushed to the back of the dresser was a flat box, a foil tray of pills sticking out the end. He picked it up and stared at the name. *Citalopram*. And there was a prescription sticker with her name on it. These had to be her antidepressants.

The toilet flushed. Derrick shoved the tablets into his pocket and hurried for the stairs.

The bathroom door opened and Charlotte walked across the landing without looking at him, humming something under her breath as she swung her door shut behind her.

Derrick went downstairs and got the glass of water. He was about to knock on her door when something occurred to him. There was something about the way Charlotte had looked: drained, spaced out, her skin an unnatural grey. It was all too familiar. Goose pimples spread over his outstretched arm.

He ducked into Mum's room and opened the wardrobe door to check if anything dangerous was missing. It was a couple of days since he'd looked, but there was even more stuff in here than before. He took stock of the medication stashed in behind the various sharp kitchen utensils. Only when he was completely sure it was all in order did he pick up the glass of water and leave it on the carpet outside her door.

That was the most he saw of her that first day. The next day, Tuesday, she only emerged to go to the loo or to grab a drink. She seemed to have stopped eating entirely. And, unless she was doing it alone in her room, there was no sign of revision.

When Mum asked him how it was going, he lied.

At first Derrick stayed glued to the window for hours at a time. There was nothing much to see except for the comings and goings of the allotment owners. The weather hadn't been much good lately, so fewer people paid a visit. It even rained for an hour or two on Tuesday afternoon. The relative stillness was almost hypnotic.

At some point, without even being conscious of it, Derrick found himself wandering away from the window a few times every hour. He would linger on the landing, trying to listen through Charlotte's door. It was always completely quiet. Not even music filtered out.

The feeling of guilt festered inside him. It filled his lungs, making it difficult to get a decent breath of air. It was the same intense worry he'd felt on the night of the incident, when he'd waited for the ambulance to show up.

Eventually he made a plate of biscuits and

summoned the courage to thump on her door. She didn't answer. He went in anyway.

'What do you think you're doing?'

Charlotte was sitting cross-legged in the corner, a revision book open in her lap. The only light came through a narrow crack in the curtain.

'You'll hurt your eyes,' he said.

'That's the least of my worries.'

Derrick pointed at the book. 'I'm supposed to be helping you with that.'

'What you're doing is the opposite of helping.'

Derrick hesitated, then thrust the plate of biscuits at her. 'I brought snacks.'

Charlotte wrinkled her nose. 'Take them away and feed them to yourself.'

'Mum said –'

'I don't care what Mum said! Get out!'

Music blared up behind him as he shut the door. Derrick went and sat on Mum's bed, ate a biscuit, and sighed. He hated dubstep.

Once it was dark he made an excuse to leave the house. In the allotments, he took a deep breath of the cool night air. Relief flooded through his entire body. He had escaped.

Someone had installed a scarecrow on their vegetable patch. There was enough light to make out its panther head, sewn together from cheap black cloth and stuffed like a teddy bear. It was a mockery. Derrick kicked it over, snapped its post in half, and ripped open the head. White fluff blew across the grass like tumbleweed.

Without his phone he didn't have a torch. Derrick skirted the patches and walked to the edge of the bushes. The family camera was stuffed into his pocket, just in case. In the darkness the overgrowth of leaves and weeds formed a solid mass, unwilling to give up its secrets.

After an hour of wandering back and forth along the line of bushes, he walked past the oak tree and rested his weight on the plastic seat of the kiddie swing. The metal frame creaked and wobbled. The seat flexed beneath his bulk.

There was only one more day before Charlotte's last exam. They hadn't done any revision together at all. It made him feel guilty, but he didn't know what more he could do. It was *her* who had barely got out of bed. It was *her* who couldn't be bothered.

The guilt wasn't because of the revision. Derrick sighed. It had been there for the last three months.

He kicked at the worn dirt carved out of the ground under the swing. The metal frame groaned. He pulled Charlotte's pills from his pocket. She didn't seem to have noticed that they'd gone. Maybe she had more. Or maybe she just didn't care.

He shouldn't have stolen them, but it wasn't as if they were doing her much good. Anyway, she wouldn't need them once he'd figured out how to catch the Beast.

The foil crackled as he popped a round white pill into his hand. Something this insignificant was supposed to save them. Derrick tossed it into his mouth and swallowed it. It stuck in his throat and he had to cough it down dry. Maybe it would make him understand what made Charlotte behave like this. What made Dad feel depressed.

Now that he knew about Dad he couldn't help thinking of times they had argued. Times Dad had lost his temper so suddenly it had frightened him. When he had helped Dad move into his flat he had accidentally dropped the microwave on the stairs. It didn't break, but Dad had shouted at him like it was the end of the world, then remained quiet and distant for the rest of the day. It was as if he'd been in a sulk or too embarrassed by his own behaviour to talk.

The shouting had always made Derrick think that Dad was strong. Maybe that wasn't the case at all.

That could all have been the depression.

The Beast would make everything clear. It had spoken to him. It would give him answers when he captured it.

There was a sudden *snap* and the straining ropes broke away from the swing seat. Derrick landed hard on his arse with an *oof*, the ropes falling across his face.

'That just about sums it up,' he muttered.

The branches of the oak tree high above him were still and immovable. It was a long time before he bothered to pick himself up.

On Wednesday morning they finally sat down together at the kitchen table surrounded by science books. One day before the exam was better late than never. Probably.

'What is the middle layer of the human heart called?'

Charlotte thought about it for a moment. Then she shook her head and slumped her chin onto her hand.

Derrick had to sound out the answer from a textbook. 'The may-o-cadium.'

'That's not right,' said Charlotte, snatching the book. 'You mean the myocardium.'

'Yeah, that. It made me think of mayonnaise.'

'This is pointless,' said Charlotte. She slammed the book shut.

'Sorry, it's getting close to lunchtime.'

'Not that! I just can't concentrate on this stuff.'

They both fell quiet for a moment. The fridge hummed behind them. Charlotte glared at the closed textbook in front of her as if she were trying to scare it into surrendering its knowledge.

Derrick attempted a nod that showed he understood. It was difficult, because he didn't understand at all. His sister looked exhausted. The rings under her eyes were like bad makeup from a horror movie.

'I just need to get through this one last thing,' said Charlotte. She slowly lowered her cheek to rest on the textbook.

'You managed the other exams all right.'

'Yeah, but I really *need* this one for my university place. I have to get accepted. It's the only thing keeping me going.'

Derrick felt a shard of fear pierce his heart. 'Do you think you'll be . . . *better* at university?'

She lifted her head to look at him. This was the first time Derrick had asked directly about her depression.

'It has to be, doesn't it?' She grabbed the textbook and flipped it open. 'It's too difficult being here.'

Derrick stared at her. He didn't know if she felt the

69

pressure that was building up inside the house. Maybe it weighed on her more than anyone.

'I'm sorry,' he said before he could stop himself.

'For what?'

'Sometimes I think . . .' He trailed off to try and find exactly the right words. It was like walking across broken glass. One wrong step would cut you open. 'Sometimes I feel guilty for finding you. You didn't want to be here any more.'

Derrick practically flinched back and waited for her to explode. But all Charlotte did was look across at him and offer the slightest of nods.

'That's why it's difficult to live here,' she said. 'This house is full of bad memories. And I'm embarrassed. More than you can possibly imagine. But you should never feel guilty about that. Never.'

They went quiet again. The fridge hummed.

It wouldn't be so easy to get rid of his guilt, Derrick knew that. But now he also knew how the trap affected her. It sealed bad memories inside the house so that she could never escape them. Maybe the only way was for her to get away to university.

Maybe the Beast being free would stop that from happening.

Charlotte grabbed the textbook and shoved it across the table at him. 'Come on, let's get back to it. Even if you are about as useful as a bag of otters.'

Derrick smiled. The guilt in his stomach had flushed away. 'They hold hands when they sleep, you know.'

'That probably won't be on the exam.'

'I know. But it's cute.'

*

The sky glowed a deep red behind long tendrils of cloud when Derrick headed out to the allotments. A few dregs of sunlight remained. It didn't matter that it was still light. He couldn't wait to escape.

After several hours of revision, Charlotte seemed to have actually absorbed some information. Her eyes grew so bloodshot that she could barely focus. It was as if concentrating for more than a few seconds took an impossible amount of effort. But she stayed calm. Even when Mum got home.

'Ready for tomorrow? I bought donuts,' Mum said.

'No, thanks,' said Charlotte. 'We'll just have to wait and see.'

Derrick would have been less worried if there'd been screaming and crying.

He strolled along to the top of the allotments track, one thumb hooked into his jogging bottoms to keep them up under the weight of the camera in his pocket. As usual he took a moment to glance around. If anyone was watching he'd just keep walking and double back.

A figure just a little further up the road caught his eye. Derrick recognised the sloping walk immediately. A thick head of greasy black hair only confirmed it: Tamoor.

A lump rose in his throat. There was nothing that should bring him down this way.

Derrick turned away from the track and hurried along the road, trying to close the distance to Tamoor. He needed to see which way he would turn. Suddenly the allotments didn't feel anywhere near as important.

Go downhill, go downhill, go downhill. Maybe he just fancied something from Tesco.

Tamoor crossed the road and turned uphill. Towards Hadley's house.

The lump in Derrick's throat swelled. He broke into a run, one hand clutching his jogging bottoms. Almost immediately a stitch jabbed between his ribs. Breathing hard, he tried to ignore it as he reached the corner and turned uphill.

Tamoor was on the other side of the road. The parked cars acted as a shield. Derrick sneaked up the hill on the opposite side.

Derrick prayed for his ex-best friend to keep walking. But Tamoor slowed down. He seemed to know exactly where he was going. Panic rose thick and hot in Derrick's chest. Words flung themselves across Derrick's memory like a malfunctioning computer screen. *Tamoor Hussein and Hadley Childs became friends.*

Tamoor brushed off the front of his shirt and swiped a hand back through his hair. Then he gave a satisfied nod and strolled up the path to ring the doorbell.

Derrick ducked low and edged along the cars until he was crouched directly opposite. He was helpless. There was nothing he could do to stop it. He watched it unfold from behind an old BMW.

He watched as Hadley opened her front door and stepped outside.

He watched her toss her red hair away from her eyes.

For just a second the light caught on her lip studs.

Then he watched as she pulled Tamoor in for a kiss.

Hand-in-hand, the two of them stepped inside the house. As the front door began to close, Derrick forced himself up. The camera was in his hand. He lifted his head just enough to take aim and captured a single shot over the roof of the car.

The front door closed him out with a sharp *bang*.

Chapter Eight

Derrick arrived back home without even remembering the walk. He stamped straight up the stairs. The camera bounced on the mattress where he threw it. He grabbed his wallet from his desk and slung an empty rucksack over his shoulder. It was always the best way to hide what he was about to do.

Back downstairs. The sound of 24-hour news drifted out into the hall from the sitting room. Problems and disasters from all over the world, churning round the house on a never-ending loop. Derrick couldn't take it. The pain in his stomach felt like it would kill him. He slammed the front door behind him, focused on the pounding of his feet on the pavement. It was all but dark outside now, a tide of deep sea blue washing across the sky. He kept his head down and his hands crammed into his pockets. It felt like his body carried him forward on auto-pilot.

Hadley and Tamoor. From somewhere deep inside him laughter tried to escape. The whole thing felt like a joke. Like life had worked out how to inflict the worst possible punishment on him. Like it was a test to see whether or not he'd break.

This could count as breaking. Or it could be the exact opposite.

At the end of the road he turned downhill. Away from *them*. The house he'd been going to for as long as he could remember. The house for which his family had a spare key. The house that he always believed would make him happy.

You're so bloody stupid. Of course she'd pick Tamoor. He's older and taller. Thinner. *You? You're just a waste of space.*

At the bottom of the hill a shortcut to Tesco took him through a small housing estate. He hurried past dirty yellow brick houses and cut into an alley.

The car park sloped down from the other side. It was almost empty this close to closing time. The supermarket was like an artless glass cathedral, parts of its shell encased in painted brickwork to try and make it look more inviting. Derrick let the automatic door acknowledge him. Then he grabbed a basket and walked under the harsh fluorescent lights.

He caught sight of the few remaining newspapers. A headline read: PANTHER ATE MY CHIHUAHUA.

The ideal route around the relevant aisles had become etched into his memory over the past few months. Every time he found himself walking it he'd swear that he would never do it again. *This is your last time. One last hurrah!*

Eight aisles along, past the pet food and alcohol. Only one or two other customers passed him, lazily pushing half-full trolleys ahead of them. No one paid him any attention. Exactly how he wanted it.

When he turned into the snack aisle the brightly coloured packages greeted him like old friends. He had lost count of how many times he had stood here since the incident. He didn't want to think about how much junk he had crammed into himself.

He swiped a big packet of crisps into his basket. Then he pivoted to grab a bag of fruit pastilles and some Maltesers. Three steps up the aisle positioned him in front of the biscuits. Two packets entered the basket. The prices added together automatically in his head and measured up against the money in his wallet. It only took a minute.

Why do you do this?

The thought came to him in a low growl. Derrick blinked it away. This wasn't the time. The whole point of this was not to think.

He walked three aisles across to the bakery. The last thing he needed was his brain staging a revolt against him. Eating was the only thing left in his life that he could control. No one held any power over it but himself. He loaded a bag of cookies and a tray of brownies into his basket, like he was loading up his problems. Gathering them all together. It wouldn't last long, but for a few hours at least his problems would be in his own hands. No one would inflict damage on him but himself.

The self-checkouts were deserted except for a member of staff leaning tiredly against the wall. She didn't seem to be watching. When he'd paid he packed it all into a carrier bag, and then stuffed that into his rucksack. Now no one would see just how much junk he'd bought.

Why do you do this?

Derrick headed for the doors. Later he would hate himself for this. There'd be no choice but to stare at his bloated reflection in the mirror. And that's exactly what he wanted.

He hurried through the alleyway. The weight of the food tugged at his back. When he reached his front door he stopped to listen for any sign of movement on the other side. Hopefully Mum would still be glued to the day's disasters on TV.

He pushed open the door and dropped the rucksack to the floor. Kicked off his shoes.

'Where've you been?'

Derrick straightened up to find Mum standing in the kitchen doorway. Instinctively he shifted his feet to make sure the rucksack was hidden behind him.

Ashamed.

'I just went for a walk.'

Mum nodded and leaned wearily against the door-frame. 'Charlotte's sleeping.'

Derrick knew that this was her way of telling him to keep quiet when he moved around the house. He answered with a nod and started up the stairs. Charlotte was pretty much the last thing he cared about right then. Nothing was more important than the junk food. He needed to stuff it into his body. The stairs creaked under his feet. He held the bag on the other side of his body, where Mum couldn't see it.

Derrick shut and locked his door behind him and dropped the rucksack onto the bed. He opened the zip and tipped it upside down. The food tumbled out along with the carrier bag. The first thing at hand was the brownies. He tore the cellophane with his fingernails and crammed the first cake whole into his mouth.

Prey.

Saliva flooded across his tongue. There was no time to savour the taste. His teeth smashed the brownie into paste. It slid down his throat before it was ready to go. The next one was already in his mouth.

The taste didn't matter. All he cared about was getting the junk food inside him.

A gnawing ache spread out from the hinges of his jaw. It forced him to chew the second brownie more slowly. With a deep sigh he sank back onto the bed. Only now did a sense of relaxation linger in his body. The rate of his thoughts slowed until there was almost nothing for his brain to focus on except chew, swallow, chew, swallow. Now he was in control. No one had power over this moment but him.

Derrick could never quite explain the feeling. Not even to himself. It wasn't about eating delicious things. It was about punishment. Shoving more fat into his body was the last thing he wanted to do, and that's exactly why he did it. It was a way to punish himself that no one else controlled. When he looked at himself in the mirror, he alone would be responsible for that pain.

It was the only time in his life when blame was obvious.

When the second brownie was in his stomach he ripped open the packet of crisps. One tip of the bag filled his mouth. The salt stung the corners of his lips. It mixed with the lingering sweetness of the brownie. For just a second his throat squeezed and he wanted to vomit. Another handful of crisps smothered the sensation.

Derrick felt something dig into the soft flesh of his back. He reached under himself and pulled out the camera. He wiped his hands on his jogging bottoms and heaved himself upright. He passed the weight of the camera from hand to hand while he chewed his mouthful into gunk and swallowed it down.

He never wanted to see the photo again. But he knew he wouldn't be able to stop himself.

He pressed the 'on' button. When the viewer lit up he found that the screen was greasy and that the image on it was blurry with movement. The clearest thing in the frame was the car roof, a red bar spread across the bottom of the photo. Hadley's house was visible just beyond it. No lights showed in the windows. That could mean her parents weren't home. He'd captured Hadley and Tamoor standing just inside the front door, hands clasped together between them. Tamoor's dark hair blended almost completely into the hallway's gloom.

Derrick shoved another handful of crisps into his mouth. Then he drove a fist down into the mattress. The crisp packet spilled over onto the floor. He ignored it and ripped open the Maltesers, shovelling them in. His eyes remained on the camera screen.

Hadley and Tamoor. It was another shitty consequence to add to all the other shitty consequences: this was what depression did. There was nothing Derrick could have done to stop it happening. It had all spun out of his control months ago. The depression at home cut him off from the rest of reality and made him powerless. It was like watching the 24-hour news: bad things endlessly piling on top of each other.

The Maltesers were almost finished before he knew it. He blinked at the empty space at the bottom of the packet, then he shifted his weight across to the desk chair. Facebook was ready and waiting when he opened his laptop. He ignored his notifications. They would be nothing but fresh abuse for not turning up at school again. Instead he went to Tamoor's profile. Tipped the rest of the chocolate into his mouth. He scrolled down the page to search for any new evidence of the relationship, but the only things on his timeline were the usual stupid pictures that his new meathead friends shared around the school. They mainly involved naked women and rubbish sex jokes.

Tamoor would never be able to keep something like this quiet.

Maybe he didn't want to hurt your feelings.

Yeah, right, like *that* was Tamoor's priority these days.

He had the only evidence he needed already, of course. For just a second he considered uploading it. He could tag them both for everyone to see. But there was no point. It would just reveal his failure to the world.

There was nothing to find on Hadley's profile either.

She didn't seem to really bother with Facebook these days. The only sign that she even knew Tamoor at all was that one-word post – *Hey*. Derrick stared at it while he chewed a mouthful of fruit pastilles. The sugar grated his tongue. It must have all happened out of sight, in private messages or whatever. Somewhere he couldn't get in the way, or try and stop it.

And now it was too late.

For the next hour he scoured Facebook for any kind of clue that he might have missed. The reserve of junk food dwindled without him even noticing it. His jaw moved mechanically. His stomach swelled in front of him. The profiles of mutual friends, strangers, shared photos he might not have seen – there was nothing to suggest that his only chance at happiness had been about to disappear.

By the time he looped back to Hadley's profile his tongue felt like a dry sponge. It was rubbed raw from all the junk that had passed across it. The corners of his mouth were split and stinging.

He clicked through her profile pictures one by one. Each of them was intimately familiar to him. Each of them felt now like a window to happiness that had closed. He went to one of her very first pictures, taken two years ago, showing Hadley, Charlotte and Derrick sitting together on a dirty cream-coloured sofa. Hadley's pet Labrador was sprawled across their laps. The massive dog had died unexpectedly last year. They were all smiling. It was the only one of her photos which featured Derrick.

After that there was one more photo with Charlotte,

before Hadley had become much stricter about what showed up on her profile. She looked perfect in every photo. She wouldn't show any other version of herself to the world.

Derrick went to his own profile. He hadn't changed the picture in months. It showed him slim and smiling – a different person.

He sighed.

Hadley and Tamoor.

A dull throb was setting in behind his eyes.

Every single time he did this, he thought the junk food – the punishment – would make him feel better. And it always did. For a little while at least. Until it came to dealing with the consequences.

At least they were consequences that he'd caused himself.

His gut felt like a balloon pumped full of water. It bulged over the waistband of his jogging bottoms. The clock on his laptop told him that it was somehow past midnight. He turned to the bed. A few biscuits were scattered across the mattress, along with some cookies and the last brownie. The crisps had been crushed into the carpet under the wheels of his desk chair.

Derrick forced himself to smile. Crumbs clung to the front of his T-shirt. His mouth felt like it had been attacked by a belt sander. The waistband of his jogging bottoms bit into his hips. He knew it would disturb his sleep. And tomorrow he'd have to face himself in the mirror. Step onto the scale. Deal with the feelings.

The rest of the junk food had to go. If he left it then he'd just end up eating it tomorrow. Once was enough.

That's what he *always* told himself, until he found himself in the alley with his hands inside the dustbin. He couldn't let that happen again.

He poured the leftovers into the carrier bag and tied it off at the top. Then he dropped it under his feet and stamped on it. The food crumbled under his weight. He walked on the spot, trying to grind it all down to nothing but dust, too ruined for him to even consider going back to it.

But he still had to get rid of it. Mum could find it when she came to empty his bin.

As quietly as he could manage he inched open his bedroom door. The house was dark. Both of the other bedroom doors were closed. Derrick crept across to the stairs, holding the carrier bag as lightly as possible to prevent it from rustling. Even with all his extra weight, he'd learned where to tread to keep the stairs from creaking.

Enough light came through the kitchen window for him to fumble for the back door handle. For some reason it wasn't locked. Mum must have forgotten. When he stepped outside the cat bolted past him into the night.

The temperature had dropped in the last couple of hours. His skin tingled in the breeze. Moisture crept into his socks as he passed the decking and hurried across the lawn. A police siren spiralled in the distance. It covered the scrape of the back gate when he tugged it open. From somewhere he caught a whiff of cigarette smoke.

In the alley he paused with one hand on the dustbin

lid. Mum might notice a carrier bag she hadn't put there herself. Several complex plans worked their way through his mind. Then he shrugged and hurled the bag as hard as he could along the alley. It sailed into the night and landed somewhere out of sight with a cushioned *thud*.

Derrick pressed his face to the cool chain-link. The allotments were still. No sign of foxes tonight. A pin-wheel turned gently in the breeze.

His eyes caught on a glimpse of light behind a flapping tarpaulin. A tiny luminescent green that made the blackness around it seem more complete. As Derrick watched, a second pinpoint of light appeared beside the first. Goose pimples scattered across his skin.

He remembered the pictures he had seen on Google. Even on his computer screen, panther eyes were piercing. Now they were staring right at him for real.

Derrick took a step away from the fence. The eyes didn't waver. As slowly as he could manage he raised a hand in something as close to a wave as his trembling arm could manage. The Beast would see it. He was sure.

The voice sounded like the night itself was trembling.

You've fattened yourself up.

It seemed to fill his whole body. Every single hair stood on end. He forced himself to look at the eyes.

'Come out. Let me see you.' Derrick wasn't sure if he spoke out loud. But the Beast heard.

That would be too easy.

And then they were gone, the sharp eyes; blink and

vanish, as if they had never existed. The tarpaulin flapped limply in the breeze. The eyes did not return.

Derrick backed his way through the gate. When he closed it behind him it felt like he hadn't breathed in minutes. Thick air filled his lungs and he almost choked. The same stifling air that filled the house. The scratch wounds were still on the gatepost. Derrick stared at them as he tried to fill his lungs. Then he started back up the garden. It felt like he was wading through treacle.

He needed a new plan. This was even more serious than he'd reckoned.

When he reached the top of the path he heard a cough from the decking. His heart jolted and he stumbled back onto the lawn. It was only then that he saw Charlotte. She was seated on one of the old white plastic garden chairs. A cigarette trailed smoke from between her fingers.

The two of them stared at each other in silence. It felt as if the night had frozen around them.

Derrick tugged at the hem of his T-shirt. 'Don't tell, ok?'

Charlotte flicked her cigarette into the nearest bush. Then she drew another from the box and held it up at him. He had had no idea that she smoked.

'I won't say anything,' he said.

A barely perceptible smile ghosted across her lips as they clamped the cigarette.

Derrick stepped back onto the path to head for the door. Before he was past the decking he stopped and stared at the paving stones under his feet. Then he turned to face her.

'What does it feel like?'

Charlotte paused with a lighter halfway to the end of her cigarette.

Derrick had Googled it once: *What does depression feel like?* There was one result that he'd always remembered.

It described depression like waking up at the dark end of a long tunnel. It said that even if you knew for sure that escape lies at the other end of the tunnel, it's impossible to get to. It's too difficult to even stand up and begin that journey. It feels hopeless, painful, like you might get lost even if you walk in a straight line. It makes you feel as if you don't even deserve to reach the other end of that tunnel.

Charlotte didn't tell him anything like this. She shrugged and said, 'Don't ruin my smoke.'

As he turned to step inside the house, Charlotte flicked the lighter. For just a moment Derrick could have sworn he saw her eyes glow green.

Chapter Nine

Derrick tried to ignore the doorbell when it shrilled through the house. He was slumped in front of the TV, hands resting on his swollen stomach, thinking about the Beast.

By the time he had got out of bed it was already mid-afternoon. His belly had ached all night and made it impossible to sleep. Some time in the early hours he had heard Charlotte come upstairs and close herself inside her room.

The sleeplessness, coupled with a throbbing food headache, made the whole night feel like a dream. The more he thought about it, the more he wondered if the green eyes had been a trick of the light, a reflection or something. And if what he'd seen weren't eyes, maybe what he'd heard wasn't a voice either. Maybe it was just his imagination.

Maybe he was going crazy.

Because this didn't *feel* like it was all in his mind. It felt more real than anything that had happened in the last three months.

The doorbell rang again and Derrick realised that,

with Charlotte upstairs and Mum washing up the dinner things, the job fell to him. He heaved himself to his feet with a groan.

In front of the bathroom mirror that morning it had looked like something was growing inside his belly. He had only managed to put one foot onto the scales before he lost his nerve.

He'd taken another of the antidepressants. *Citalopram* – he'd Googled it and got a long list of possible side effects. But he didn't feel any different at all. They were useless.

About an hour after he got up, Charlotte arrived home from her final exam. She can't have slept at all. There was no drama; no tears, doors slamming, broken ornaments – nothing at all like he had expected. She just put her bag down and unlaced her shoes. Derrick had had to hurry to think of something to say. Everything he'd practised was in case it went badly.

'It's all over, then,' was the best he could manage.

She'd looked at him like he was the worst kind of idiot.

Before he reached the front door he stopped to adjust his T-shirt (XXXL, the biggest he owned, the one he always wore after a junk food session). Keeping the damage hidden away from other people meant the guilt was all his. The guilt that he hated. The guilt that he needed.

He opened the door to find Hadley, in the middle of pulling her hair back into a loose ponytail. She beamed at him, smoothing loose red strands away from her eyes. His heart jolted to his gullet. The evening was warm, and matched by her black tank top and shorts. Bright pink studs shone on her bottom lip.

'Oh, hi, Derrick!'

Derrick swallowed. Usually he only saw her when their families got together. That usually gave him several days in advance to plan exactly what he would say and how he would behave. Spontaneity wasn't exactly his strong suit. The thought of how fat he must look made him want to slam the door in her face and run.

'Can I come in?'

'Sorry, yeah.'

Derrick stepped aside and watched her move past him into the hall. He should hate her after what he had seen last night. His feelings for her should have evaporated – she was tainted by Tamoor now. But as she fixed him with a quizzical look he felt heat flood into his cheeks. And into somewhere lower. It hadn't changed: she was still everything he wanted. He needed her more than ever.

The sight of her smooth, bare legs made his stomach flip.

'Who is it?' shouted Mum from the kitchen.

'Hi, Karen!' Hadley shouted back.

'Oh, Hadley! How's your mum?' Without waiting for an answer Mum poked her head around the kitchen door. 'That's such an old-lady thing to ask, isn't it?'

Hadley laughed. The sound of it made Derrick's heart flutter. 'Remember, you're two years younger than my mum.'

'That's why I like you, Hadley.' Mum pulled her head back out of sight. 'Charlotte's upstairs.'

'Thanks!' Hadley turned to face Derrick and dropped her voice to a whisper. 'But I need to speak to you first.'

Derrick had never known his heart could do a back-flip. Variations of those exact words had kicked off every fantasy he'd ever had about her. They probably numbered somewhere in the millions by now.

She nodded for him to follow her into the sitting room. As soon as she was through the door, Derrick slapped himself hard across the face. The sting jolted his brain. *She's not exactly going to declare her unbridled love for you, is she?* The thought of what she might say instead sent a chill of fear down his spine. She could have seen him outside her house last night. Looking at her Facebook profile was a lot less terrifying than facing the real thing.

'I found your phone,' she said quietly as she reached into her shorts pocket.

She handed it over. The screen was cracked, an almost perfectly straight fracture from top to bottom. Dirt had ground itself down into the fissure. But at least the screen still lit up when he swiped his thumb across it.

'My dad found it, actually. On his vegetable patch,' said Hadley. A hint of a smile played around her lips. 'Don't worry, he didn't know it's yours.'

'How did *you* know it was mine?'

Derrick's mind raced through everything on his phone. Tried to pinpoint anything that might incriminate him.

'I looked at the photos. There's loads of your cat.'

'Oh.' That was probably worse than if she'd found something dodgy.

'So how did it get there?'

She perched on the arm of the sofa. Derrick swallowed hard and compelled his eyes to stay away from her legs. Instead he tried to focus on the pair of piercings in her bottom lip. The pink studs gleamed like exaggerated extensions of her flesh.

He scrambled for something to tell her. The truth wasn't exactly convincing. It would just make him sound like he was going crazy.

Maybe you are going crazy.

He didn't want to tell her about the Beast. The realisation was sudden but steadfast. For whatever reason the panther had escaped, it was up to him to capture it. That was his duty now. If Hadley got involved it would only complicate things. No, Hadley had to be kept away from all this. She seemed so miraculously . . . unaffected. Even though she was the only person Charlotte had ever told about the incident, somehow she hadn't caught the disease like everything else. Derrick had to make sure she stayed that way.

'I was just out for a walk,' he said, dropping his eyes to the battered phone in his hand. 'I must've dropped it.'

'You know you're not allowed in there.' Hadley wagged her finger. 'The owners will straight up shoot you.'

Derrick grinned. 'There are places out there where nobody can see you. I'll show you sometime.'

He felt his cheeks burn. He hadn't even meant it as anything flirty and it still came out wrong. He'd made it sound like he was going to kill her or something.

Hadley's eyebrows creased into a frown. She sprung up from the sofa arm and cleared her throat. 'Is it ok to go up and see Charlotte? Did her exam go all right?'

Derrick answered quickly. 'Fingers crossed, she seems fine.'

She may have been immune to the film of depression that had coated everything in his life, but Hadley had never quite got the hang of how to tiptoe around Charlotte. They'd been friends their entire lives, but there was no way the relationship could have survived intact. It was like making friends with a landmine.

Hadley flashed him a knowing smile. 'Awesome. Maybe I'll catch you before I go.'

Derrick stayed in the sitting room and listened to the stairs creak delicately under her feet. A trace of her perfume lingered on the air. He leaned to breathe it in deep. He had no idea what smell perfume was supposed to replicate. Flowers or something. To him it smelled of a thrilling freedom.

He sunk back onto the sofa and swiped his phone to life. The cracked screen felt sharp under his thumb. Even though it had been gone for several days there were no new messages. Maybe he wasn't even popular enough to receive abuse any more. Derrick sighed and scrolled through his photos instead. Just to check what Hadley might have seen. The photo reel contained 18 photos. Fifteen of them were of the cat. The cat asleep on the windowsill; the cat asleep on the microwave; the cat staring at him wondering why he was taking her bloody photo again while she was trying to sleep.

If Hadley wasn't impressed by you before, she's bound to be now.

At the very end of the reel was a video. The static image was completely black aside from an orange smudge across the middle. He tapped the play button with his thumb. It was only when the image started moving, and the muffled sound of heavy breathing kicked in, that he remembered what it was: the video he had recorded when he chased the Beast across the allotments. He'd forgotten all about it.

It was nothing but a shaky blur of black and brown. The image rocked side to side, to the percussion of his feet hitting the grass. The Beast could have been right in front of the camera for all he knew – visibility was zero.

Suddenly the images lurched sideways and flipped over. As this happened, some details actually began to become clearer. With an *oof!* of his body hitting the ground, the frame settled on a patch of cropped grass, and became illuminated by orange light, presumably from the houses nearby where he fell. Next, he heard the sound of his breathing become distant, and remembered how he'd stumbled back to his feet in the hope of catching up with the Beast. Quiet settled over the video then. Over an hour remained on the runtime. It had kept recording until the memory ran out.

Derrick dropped the phone into his lap. The video was useless.

He was just guiding his finger to stop the video when something moved across the image. He fumbled the phone back into his grip and swiped the screen to rewind it a few seconds. Then he held the cracked glass up to his face.

A dark shape passed over the grass. Derrick jabbed to pause it. In the low orange light it was almost impossible to make out. The shadow didn't look completely solid. Slivers of light broke through it. At the bottom of the screen it was unblemished. Thinner strips stretched up from it. Derrick carefully edged his finger across the screen. The video rolled slowly forward. The strips seemed to move at odd angles to one another.

It was the shadow of legs, upside down. Four legs moving quickly just above the camera shot. And they belonged to something big.

He wasn't going crazy. The Beast had been there.

He sprang up from the sofa. He couldn't work out what to do first. The sensible choice would be to upload it to his computer and check it out on a bigger screen. But he was way too excited to be sensible. His first thought was – Charlotte.

He ran for the stairs. It was *proof*. He had trapped the Beast inside his phone. Maybe it would be enough to break the siege on their lives. If he exposed the panther, showed the world that it was *real*, then its freedom – its power – would be gone.

He climbed, adjusted his T-shirt to be sure it was properly covering his stomach. He couldn't show Hadley any of this, of course. He would get Charlotte alone, ask her to come to his room.

He went to knock on her bedroom door.

'It's disgusting!' Charlotte's voice, filled with anger.

Derrick froze. It was a tone of voice he'd heard a million times before.

'What would you even know about it?' Hadley spat back.

'He used to be round here all the time! He's two years younger than you!'

'A year and a half!'

'Oh yeah, that makes it much better.'

Derrick retreated behind his own doorframe. They were arguing about Tamoor. It was something he definitely shouldn't be eavesdropping on, but there was no way he was going to stop.

'Why do you even care?'

'You know what he did to my brother, right?'

Hadley went quiet at that. Panic flickered in Derrick's chest. Hadley might have seen the video before it was taken down. Tamoor could have shown her the original, on his phone. Embarrassment blazed through his entire body at the thought.

'It's a betrayal.' Charlotte's voice was quieter now. Firmer.

'What are you on about?'

'Derrick saved my life. You know that. And your new *boyfriend* treats him like a piece of shit!'

'So what?' Hadley shouted back, her voice only getting louder. 'God, I knew you were crazy, but I didn't realise it had got this bad.'

Silence fell. The tension was suddenly so thick that it seemed to bleed out through the gap underneath the door. Derrick recognised that silence. He braced himself for the –

'I'm not crazy.'

'Look –'

'I'M NOT CRAZY.'

Derrick recoiled. From downstairs came the sound of a plate being dropped. Mum's footsteps moved towards the bottom of the stairs.

'Get out.'

'Charlotte, I didn't mean –'

'I SAID GET OUT!'

The door handle rattled. Derrick ducked back into his room. Hadley stormed past, her ponytail bobbing as she hurried down the stairs. He heard her mutter something to Mum before the front door slammed shut.

Derrick stepped reluctantly onto the landing. He found his sister standing in the middle of her room, hands clenched into fists.

'Did you know?' she said.

Derrick nodded. 'Yesterday.'

They stood and looked at each other. It was just like last night. Derrick found himself searching for the green flash in her eyes. Now they just looked dark and tired.

'Everything ok up there?' called Mum from the bottom of the stairs.

Derrick took a step inside her room. 'Why did you stand up for me?'

'I don't need a reason.' She shrugged. 'That's the advantage of being crazy.'

Derrick nodded without even knowing why. He looked at his sister, then over at her collection of tiny fragile figurines. He looked at the phone, still clutched in his hand. It didn't seem right to show her now, somehow, so he shoved it down into his pocket.

It wasn't far from dark when Derrick stepped outside into the garden. The sun was on the other side of the house. It cast a long, impenetrable shadow across the patio and lawn.

Derrick walked onto the grass and lowered himself down until he was sitting cross-legged. The cat ran out from under the bushes and rubbed up against his knees.

When he left Charlotte's room his stomach began to hurt so much he thought he was going to vomit. Even now it squeezed inside his gut and made him flinch. He tried to focus on the softness of the cat's fur instead.

As soon as it was night-dark he would go into the allotments and think of a way to find the Beast again. Things were getting worse every single day. The house was going to suffocate them.

Charlotte was beginning to lose it again. He could tell. It was just like before – and just like before, he was the only one who could do something about it. It wasn't enough to capture the panther on video. It wouldn't be so easy.

As he looked up at the back gate, something caught his eye. Midway along the garden fence, the bushes had been torn open. Leaves and branches scattered the path.

Derrick heaved himself up. The cat followed on his heels as he walked cautiously over to inspect the damage.

The bushes had been shredded, raggedly so – not with tools. Tattered leaves and twisted stems still clung to the branches. It looked as if . . .

It looked like it had been done with claws.

He glanced down at the cat, who was dutifully sniffing the area. 'This wasn't you, was it?'

He reached into the ripped-open hole. Behind it, deep scratches marked the fence. Long vertical slivers of wood carved away just like the damage on the back gatepost.

The Beast had marked more of its territory.

And this time it was closer to the house.

Chapter Ten

Before he jumped the gate, Derrick carefully scanned the allotments to check if anyone was still around – some people would work on their patches right up until the last of the light was almost gone. The sky glowed orange as the sun descended behind the houses at a crawl. It was still warm enough for sweat to bead on his forehead. Even with his face pressed to the chain-link he could barely see to the far end of the allotments, where the warehouse sat.

Well, there was no one near the gate at least. He heaved himself up and dropped over the other side as softly as he could manage. Which wasn't very softly at all.

The allotments were quiet. They *always* seemed quiet. It felt almost as if it all existed just for him. The plants and vegetables flourished while everything else in his life was withering. He reached out a hand to a creeper that had wound itself around a bamboo pole, but flinched his hand away at the last moment. His touch might kill it. He felt contagious.

The fresh air made him feel light-headed. The pain

in his stomach had evaporated as soon as he jumped over the gate.

He walked straight towards the thick bushes and nettles that choked the back fence. A number of plans occurred to him. For instance, he could smother himself in meat juice to lure the Beast out, and then wrestle it into submission. It was a plan that might carry one or two major risks.

What he really needed was some kind of sophisticated hunting equipment. The most useful thing he owned was a pair of handcuffs. That would definitely involve a spot of panther wrestling.

The video on his phone wasn't enough. The marks on the fence were proof of that. They were closer to the house than before. It almost felt like the Beast was mocking him, rubbing its freedom in his face by marking his garden as its territory.

The overgrown mess of the bushes was the perfect place for a panther to hide. It was from here he'd seen it leap when he chased it.

He swiped his phone to light it up and aimed it at the ground, then he walked along the edge of the overgrowth. Now and again he had to step over piles of scrap wood ready for the bonfire, or around discarded garden furniture. There were too many places where the leaves had been flattened or hollows opened up where something could sleep. Any one of them could have been made by the Beast.

A little way past the oak tree he reached a patch of ground at the edge of the bushes where the grass had been worn down to dirt to form a crude path. The overgrowth seemed thinner here. The pale light from his phone pushed right through it. It seemed to trail right back to the fence. It might be a fox path; it might be a path for something bigger.

Derrick crouched and held the phone closer to the ground. The earth was still damp from the recent rain, a mess of paw prints scattered across it. The light threw them into sharp relief. He ran his fingertips gently over the marks. Only a couple were completely intact, most of them partial or overlapping. They reminded him of the prints his cat would trail across the kitchen floor when she came inside from the wet, only they were bigger. *Much* bigger.

His knees began to ache. With a twinge of pain he straightened up. The phone's ghostly light reached through the scraggly branches. He could just make out a definite path cutting all the way through to the fence and, slightly wide of that path, a wooden crate, half swallowed by weeds.

It looked damp and rotten. It had clearly been abandoned a long time ago. He shoved forward into the bushes. Branches and nettles clawed at his waist. One side of the crate was missing, leaving it open like a poorly made dog kennel. It would easily be big enough for a panther to get inside and curl up to sleep.

If the Beast was in there, there was no way it could have missed him approaching. He wasn't exactly light on his feet.

'Are you there?' he said. It didn't feel strange to talk to it. Here in the allotments was the only place he had heard its voice.

There was no reply. He took a deep breath, placed his free hand on top of the crate, and leaned down to peer inside.

A musty smell of rotting wood hit his nostrils. The crate was empty. A nastier smell made him flinch back. The only thing his phone's white light picked out was a dark, wet lump.

Panther poo.

Derrick eagerly held his phone over it and snapped a picture. He could Google it later to make sure.

He straightened up and looked around him. It would be embarrassing if the Beast saw what he was doing.

He waded out of the bushes and walked across to the grass underneath the oak tree. He shifted his weight down and sat with his back against it. The night air felt warm in his lungs.

Across from him, he saw the bathroom light blaze on in his house. He was so close to the chaos that was trapped within; but out here he could still feel peaceful. He leaned his head back against the hard tree trunk. He knew it couldn't last for ever. The allotments were surrounded by the darkness on three sides now: home ahead of him, the shell of the warehouse to one side, and Hadley's place just a little way up the hill. Places where it was impossible to escape the destruction wrought by depression, places sealed away from the rest of the world.

If he could catch the Beast, Charlotte would be able to escape . . .

Do you smell blood?

He woke up with a jolt, slumped sideways onto the grass. A chill ran through his bones. How long had he slept? He swiped his phone to life. The clock showed that he'd been out here for over two and a half hours. That would be hard to explain.

He stumbled to his feet and adjusted his T-shirt. Then he aimed the phone back into the bushes for the final time. The crate still appeared to be unoccupied.

The Beast hadn't eaten him while he slept. He hurried for the gate, not eager to try his luck.

Every downstairs light was on when he pushed the front door open. That meant Mum was probably still awake. His repertoire of excuses was running dry. He'd been gone too long for anyone to believe he'd been out for a jog, not long enough to constitute a plausible kidnapping, and it wasn't exactly like he had friends to visit any more.

The quietness of the house interrupted his thoughts. It felt unnatural. Silence, when it fell inside the house, was always thick with tension. But this . . . this felt new. Absolute. Empty.

Something was wrong.

Derrick poked his head around the sitting room door. The TV was off, the floor lamp shining over the empty sofa. He moved on to check the kitchen and froze in the doorway. Cutlery and shards of broken plate were scattered across the floor. The plastic draining board beside the sink had been flipped over.

A single jagged spike of china lay on the table, smeared with blood.

Derrick ran for the stairs. Something terrible had happened while he was out. *You were only gone for a few hours.* They could be at the hospital. But no one had tried to call him.

Upstairs, every light was on except for his own. He ran to Charlotte's room. It was empty. Her bedclothes were kicked into a ball on the floor. He turned and hurried into Mum's room.

He stopped dead inside the door. A heavy sigh of relief emptied out his lungs. Mum and Charlotte were asleep together on the bed, arms wrapped around each other. Derrick saw straight away that both of them were breathing. Mum's forearm was bandaged with a white hand towel. It was red where spots of blood seeped through.

Derrick took a step closer. He'd only left the house for a few hours and things had got worse. It was impossible. He couldn't be here all the time to make sure something like this didn't happen. There were too many things he had to do.

The wardrobe door hung open, and an array of Charlotte's university stuff spilled out – that's where the towel on Mum's arm had come from. They could have been arguing about university. These days it seemed to be the only thing they all had in common: getting Charlotte to university.

He stood and watched them sleep for a long time. The relief that had flooded his body made it hard to move his legs. When finally he went back downstairs he headed for the kitchen, gingerly tiptoed through the debris, and retrieved a dustpan and brush from underneath the sink. The cat appeared behind him and hopped up onto the table.

'Careful,' said Derrick, pointing down at the shattered plates. The cat stared at him like he was an idiot.

Just then he caught his reflection in the glass of the back door. The glare of the fluorescent light overhead blotted out the view of the garden. The window was nothing but a black mirror. He studied the roundness of his stomach, prodded a finger into his soft flesh. He adjusted his waistband and let a long sigh escape from somewhere deep inside him.

It was his responsibility to stop this. But he didn't know how.

He dropped to the floor. Small fragments of crockery ground into his knees as he swept up the mess. It took several journeys to the bin before he was satisfied. Next, he collected up the cutlery from every corner of the room. There were still no knives. He put it all away in the drawer. The cat stared at him accusingly.

'Don't tell anyone I didn't wash them,' whispered Derrick.

The cat jumped from the table to the counter top that faced the back window. Derrick dropped the last of the forks into place.

Lastly, he came to the bloodied spike on the table. It didn't look like a lot of blood. There wasn't a puddle or anything, just a rusty smear across the plate, a couple of droplets on the tabletop. He grabbed several pieces of paper towel and wiped it away. Then he swaddled the shard in the paper and took it to the bin.

He didn't want to think about what might have happened. The possibilities were too terrible.

As he dropped it into the bin the cat gave a strained *mewl* from behind him.

'Shut it, cat.'

He turned around to find her standing tense on the counter top. Her back was arched and her fur had fluffed itself up into a ball. Her eyes were fixed on the window.

Derrick felt his whole body go numb. 'What is it?'

The cat hissed in reply. A sharp rasp that sent goose bumps skittering across Derrick's skin. The cat never behaved this way. Usually she was too stupid to react to anything at all.

There was something outside the window, hidden behind the glare of the overhead light. Derrick forced himself to take a step forward. He held his breath tight in his lungs. The cat backed away slowly in the opposite direction, retreating along the countertop. Derrick took another step. The glass showed nothing but their reflections. His eyes were wide and startled, like a prey animal too frightened to run.

When he was as close as he dared, he leaned towards the glass. The breath lodged in his lungs began to ache, but he couldn't quite manage to release it. His forehead touched the window and its coldness shocked him. The breath erupted out and fogged the glass.

Hurriedly he wiped it away and pushed his eyes as close as possible. As the glare of the light receded, the garden came plainly back at him, rested under a blanket of night. The top of the path. The decking. The stretch of lawn before the back fence. Empty. He looked for a long time before he finally straightened up and turned. The cat had fled.

'Stupid animal,' said Derrick, surprised by how much his voice shook.

He returned his gaze to the window.

It had been there, dark and powerful and hidden, looking in at them all. Seeing and unseen.

Derrick suddenly felt very cold.

Chapter Eleven

When the crying stopped, Charlotte seemed to shut down entirely. For weeks he never saw her smile or laugh or frown. Her face was completely impassive at all times. It was as if the depression had clamped around her and nothing from the outside world could break through.

Mum said it was the medication that the doctor gave her. The pills she had to take every morning. The pills that were now hidden in his room. Derrick had heard people call them *happy pills*, but they couldn't be more wrong. The medication didn't make her happy. It made her absolutely flat. It messed up her sleeping, too. Derrick remembered being woken up most nights by the sound of her door opening, the gentle murmur of her music through the wall. He used to shove the pillow over his head and thump on the wall dividing their rooms, but she didn't seem to notice. If she did, then she didn't care. He had hated her for that.

The explosions of crying began when Charlotte started going back to school. As far as he knew she managed to bottle it all up for weeks at a time. Then the despair would pour out of her for hours straight.

Derrick had spent those nights downstairs, as far away from the noise as possible. There had been nothing but anger and resentment then. The guilt and the fear only came afterwards.

The doctor changed her medication and referred her to therapy. The waiting list was twelve months long.

Too long.

The high street was quiet during school hours. A couple of elderly ladies shuffled between shops, leaning on their trollies for support. A small group of men stood at a bus stop and stared into space. Derrick tugged at the hem of his T-shirt. No one paid him any attention as he passed the loan shops and pound stores. Their windows were filled with cheap plastic panther toys and artistically bankrupt framed posters.

He had woken up with intense pain in his stomach. It felt as if his gut would rupture. It was time to step up his hunt. Every time he thought of the Beast peering into his house a shiver ran down his spine.

The butcher's shop was at the top end of the high street, tucked between a phone-unlocking stall and an empty unit. An old-fashioned red-and-white-striped awning stretched out to cover the entrance. It obscured a window filled with garish hunks of red meat.

The air inside was cold from the ice that filled the display counters. Derrick leaned his elbows on the chilled glass. There were a few steaks laid out across the ice, and beside them a plastic sack of dark red mush, like blood jelly. Business didn't exactly seem to be booming. From somewhere out back came the blunt thud of a cleaver slamming into a chopping board.

The idea had struck him that morning. He woke up remembering the picture of Hadley with her old Labrador. They used to keep it in a cage when no one was home. A *big* cage.

'All right, Derrick?'

Derrick looked up to see Hadley's dad step out of the back room. Despite his chosen lifestyle, he'd never been much of an advert for organic living. A blue apron didn't quite manage to hide a stubborn beer belly. Elsewhere the skin on his arms and neck sagged away from the bone, like the flesh inside had melted. Derrick could never quite work out how Hadley had this man for a dad.

'Hi, Mr Childs.'

'I didn't expect to find you out here. Everything all right at home?'

Derrick nodded and squeezed his mouth into something that approximated a smile. No one knew about their problems like Hadley's family did. It should have been a relief. It should have given him somebody to talk to. Instead it just seemed to make things uncomfortable.

A strained silence settled between them. Eventually Hadley's dad broke it.

'Good. What can I do you for?'

Derrick straightened up and rested his palms flat on the counter. 'Do you still have your old dog cage?'

'I think so, in the conservatory.'

'Any chance I can borrow it?'

Hadley's dad folded his arms across his chest. The skin folded up like half-melted cheese. 'I don't see why not. What do you need it for?'

Derrick was ready for this. 'School summer project,' he said, almost too quickly.

'Say no more. No one's home at the moment, but you can let yourself in and take it.'

Now Derrick managed a real smile. 'Also, I need a couple of cheap steaks.'

'Some off-cuts do you?'

Derrick nodded. Hadley's dad went off to the back room. The rustle of thick paper being folded around something drifted through to the front of the shop.

He returned with a small package, wrapped like a takeaway sandwich. He dropped it on the counter with a flourish.

'Free of charge, as it's for your education and all. Get them in the fridge quick, mind. It won't take long for them to turn in this weather.'

'Thanks, Mr Childs.' Derrick grabbed the package and turned for the door. He'd been expecting a pang of guilt for lying, but nothing came. 'You have a patch on the allotments behind our house, right?'

Hadley's dad answered with a nod.

'Have you ever seen anything . . . weird out there?'

'Weird?' He scratched at a fold of flesh underneath his chin. 'Depends what you mean, really. I never saw this panther they keep banging on about. The other day I found a mobile phone in with my lettuces.'

'Ok, never mind!' Derrick hurried for the door.

'Go careful now!'

111

Derrick shoved the package into his pocket and hurried along the high street. It was only mid-morning but the temperature had already begun to soar. His armpits were starting to sweat.

That morning, he'd gone downstairs just in time to catch Mum as she finished breakfast. The sleeves of her suit jacket now covered her arms, but when she'd reached down for her shoes Derrick had caught a glimpse of the bandage wrapped close to the elbow. Neither of them mentioned how few plates and bowls were left in the kitchen.

'Keep an eye on her, ok?' Mum had said before she ran for her train.

As Derrick reached the corner he fished into his pocket and pulled out a fistful of keys. He untangled his own and picked out a set simply labelled *SPARE*. It had been a safe bet that Hadley's dad wouldn't refuse. Even if he had, Derrick would have taken it anyway.

It was hard to be certain, but Derrick was pretty sure he could remember the first time he was ever taken to Hadley's house. The plastic cover was over his push-chair. Fat drops of rain pattered just inches from his face. More trees lined the hill then, some with branches so low that Mum had to duck.

Back then he had been wheeled to the front door and Mum had rung the bell. Now, Derrick used the key. His sweaty palms smelled of copper. The lock clicked back and Derrick shoved the door open.

Not only was it the first time he'd ever been inside her house on his own, it was also the first time he'd been near it since he'd seen Tamoor go inside.

Everything was exactly as he remembered. A shoe rack just inside the door where he used to leave his trainers spilled footwear over the worn green carpet. A wireless router flickered on a shelf mounted not-quite-straight on the wall. Its red and blue lights flashed across the old family portrait, made when Hadley was a toddler. Her head looked approximately the same shape as a melon. They had always laughed about it. A few months ago he had put it on Facebook and tagged her, but she demanded he take it down.

It all felt different in the hush. Usually he walked in with his family to the sound of greetings and drinks offered, the TV on, or maybe some music. Now it was silent. It felt like there should at least be a clock ticking – just something reassuring. It made him feel like an invader. He hated it.

The emptiness made him move quickly. At the end of the hallway he turned into the dining room at the back of the house. This is where they used to spend most of their visits. Their parents would get drunker and drunker until they stopped caring that he and Hadley were sneaking drinks of their own.

He squeezed past the dining table, stacked high with books and loose scraps of paper, to the conservatory at the back. The door was already half open, heat from the dirty glass box slipping into the room and stifling the air.

It slid the rest of the way open with a protesting rasp. The damp smell of earth inside made him recoil. It was the same smell as the allotments, but concentrated

113

inside the tiny space. Plant pots of all different sizes were arranged around the glass walls. Some contained nothing but soil, while others sprouted elaborate leaves and flowers. The damp air condensed on the glass and made it feel like he was breathing underwater.

The dog cage was hidden behind a row of vacant clay pots. Derrick shifted them out of his way, and then threaded his fingers through the wire mesh of the cage. The metal pinched at his fingers. His muscles burned when he heaved it up. It took a strange sideways shuffle to manoeuvre it through the door and rest it against the dining table. He sucked in a deep breath of air but the heat just made him splutter.

Mud had somehow smeared itself across his fingers. Derrick studied the brown smudges. Then he adjusted his T-shirt, secured a solid grip on the cage and wrestled it into the hallway.

He propped it beside the front door, then turned back for the dining room. It was only polite to put back everything he had moved. When he passed the bottom of the stairs the silence of the house seemed to swallow him. Pain gripped his stomach. It wasn't the same here any more. Now that he recognised it he wanted to cry. Depression seemed to drift through the air like sediment dropping to the bottom of a river.

Derrick rested a hand on the banister. He looked up the stairs. Cool air drifted down from the gloomy landing.

The house would stay empty for hours. This was an opportunity he might never have again.

The stairs didn't creak like they did at home. *They*

haven't had to put up with your weight. He climbed softly, as if someone might be listening out for him.

You shouldn't do this.

When he reached the landing he paused. There were no windows to allow in any sunlight. Every door was closed. His eyes settled on the door directly opposite the stairs. Patches of bare wood littered the white paint-work like bruises. Derrick remembered the stickers that used to decorate it. They had been all flowers and stars and girly stuff. Torn off as soon as she grew out of them.

Derrick rested a hand against the wood and turned his head. He pressed his ear to the door. Even though he knew it was empty he felt his heart begin to race.

One push made the door swing smoothly inwards under its own weight.

The warm, exotic scent hit him immediately. It was the smell of Hadley's hair. It made his skin tingle.

Derrick took a deep breath of it. The door knocked against the wall and made him jump. He caught his reflection in the floor-length mirror directly opposite.

You shouldn't be here.

His reflected self stared back at him, eyes brimming with shame. But it stepped forward with him into the room all the same.

The curtains were still drawn. A crack in the middle sent a sharp sliver of sunlight cutting across the middle of the room. Everything inside felt different now that he was here alone, even though he'd been here dozens of times before. The chequered sofa piled high with clothes where he'd slept years ago, that night when Mum was away at work. Next to the door was the

115

dresser, stained with makeup. Littered across its top were perfume bottles, hair stuff, a plastic box overflowing with jewellery. The floor was littered with empty drinks bottles and stray hair bands.

The bed was tucked into the corner. A single, unmade. The sheet still wrinkled where she'd rolled off it that morning. Heat flushed underneath Derrick's skin. Even though the room was cool he could feel sweat bead on his forehead. He took a step deeper into the room. His heart thudded in his chest. He wanted to climb into her bed and breathe the smell of her pillow. He wanted to scour every inch of the sheets for any sign of Tamoor.

This is what he was fighting for.

This room is where he would be happy.

But not if you're here alone.

Her tablet rested beside the pillow. Before he could stop himself he flipped back the cover and the screen came to life. There was no password required, just a screen full of apps. Immediately he opened her email. But she had signed out, and he couldn't even guess what her login details might be.

He was about to give up when another thought occurred to him. He opened Facebook and it went straight into her homepage. He tapped open her private messages. This was how Tamoor had contacted her. Maybe it would give him some answers.

There it was, right at the top of the list. Derrick took a breath. Then he opened the messages.

There were hundreds. They must have chatted for hours. The sight of it made him feel sick. It was suddenly difficult to focus on what they said. It all just looked like stupid flirting. The sort of stuff he would never be brave enough to say to her himself. He scrolled rapidly through them. There was only one thing he wanted to see: his own name. He wanted to know that they'd at least thought about him.

Nothing. The screen fell still when he reached the first message. It was from Hadley. She had sent the opening message after he posted on her timeline. All it said was *Hey yourself.*

The shaft of sunlight seemed to burn his skin. He turned suddenly and rushed out of the room. The door slammed behind him. It felt like there was a hot coal in his stomach.

He let his feet thump hard on the stairs and threw the front door open so that it bashed into the wall. It left a dent in the wallpaper. It was only when he reached for the cage that it occurred to him it was too heavy to lift over the allotment gate.

He spun to face the shelf where the router flickered over unopened post and takeaway leaflets. He ran his hand along it until he found a set of keys half fallen into the gap between the shelf and the wall. A set of keys labelled *ALLOTMENTS.*

It took ten minutes just to drag the cage down the hill. It had always been Derrick's hope that, somewhere beneath all the fat, all of his eating would have fed some pretty decent muscles. The intense burning in his arms and shoulders suggested otherwise. By the time he reached the allotments track he just let the cage drag through the dirt.

Droplets of sweat landed in expanding circles on his T-shirt. At the gate he let the cage drop and fished the padlock key out of his pocket. As he opened it up, he glanced around the patches. A few people were about, working on their plots further down the allotments. With a cage in tow it might look like he was helping someone out with their patch. Hopefully no one would pay him any attention.

He gripped the mesh between his fingers and dragged the cage around the patches and beyond the oak tree. It churned up the grass behind him. At the edge of the bushes he let it drop. Mud and mangled leaves had caught in the wire. He swiped the sweat from his forehead. The allotments didn't feel so peaceful in the glaring sunlight. It didn't feel so easy to relax. It felt like the people around him were trespassing on his territory.

Moving quickly he unhooked the clips that kept the cage folded flat. The whole thing pulled up into a box shape. The sides wedged in place to hold it upright. Then he squeezed the clips back into place.

It was about the same size as the wooden crate. The cage door was a loose panel that slid directly up through a slot in the roof of the wire. Derrick lifted it up and tried to balance it open. As soon as he let it go it slammed back into place. The impact sang through the metal. Derrick's immediate plan was to kick it. Then he actually thought about it and scraped up a tiny ball of damp soil from under his feet. Now when he opened the door he wedged it in place with the mud. The panel stayed open. Derrick shook the cage with his hands, and then stood up and practised his original plan of kicking it. The jolt made the door snap shut.

Next he waded into the bushes until he reached the wooden crate. He leaned in to make sure it was still empty, and then wedged his hands underneath it. Cold dirt dug into his fingernails. The overgrown weeds tried to hold it in place, but Derrick tore them loose as he levered the crate up and rolled it away. The dried lump of poo inside clattered like a stone in a washing machine.

Once the crate had reached the back fence, Derrick turned it so that the open side was blocked by the wood. Now the cage would be the best hiding option available.

The crate had left a square patch of flattened ground underneath it. Insects skittered across it in frenzied bids for escape. Derrick retrieved the cage and, with the weight of it wedged against his belly, shuffled it into the empty space. Then he rigged the door and stepped back to admire his handiwork.

When he'd caught his breath he pulled the white paper package from his pocket. The meat had already turned warm and slimy from the weather. There were two lumps of greyish red flesh, cut through with white veins of fat. It was probably the same quality of meat that went into cat food anyway. Derrick lowered himself onto all fours and slipped the flesh right to the back of the cage.

The Beast would go inside to grab the meat. When it tried to turn around in the narrow space it would knock the cage and *snap!* The door would drop shut.

Then he would have captured the Beast. It would return their freedom to them. Charlotte would go to university and he could begin to fix everything that had broken.

It wasn't a perfect plan. He had to admit that. But it was the best he'd got. He could keep watch from the back of his house with the binoculars.

The pain in his stomach diminished a little. The cage would work. It *had* to work.

Derrick tugged at the surrounding weeds and bushes to try and conceal the trap. There was some scrap wood nearby and he piled it around the sides of the cage. From the edge of the bushes it looked no more conspicuous than the crate had.

All he had to do now was come back later and claim his pet panther. His prize.

Chapter Twelve

The allotments remained largely empty for most of the day, even with the uninterrupted sunshine overhead. Maybe it was too hot for old people to risk being outside. Or maybe they were worried about becoming an afternoon snack. Derrick stood at the back window and swept the binoculars between the vegetable patches. A middle-aged woman in stained dungarees tugged up weeds and chucked them into a crooked wheelbarrow. Later in the afternoon a van pulled up. Kids spilled out and ran to the swing set. They burst into tears when they found it broken.

Oops.

No one seemed to notice the cage. It was almost directly in line with the window, and Derrick could frame it perfectly in the binocular lenses. Even though the Beast wasn't likely to come for it before nightfall, he wanted to keep an eye on it anyway. Just in case.

The sun gradually arced to the front of the house as the afternoon stretched on. Long shadows pushed themselves across the allotments.

The phone began to ring downstairs. Derrick ignored

it, happy to let it ring out – but to his surprise there was the sound of Charlotte's door opening and he heard her trot downstairs. The ringing cut off, and he forgot about it, a sudden urge to check inside the wardrobe overcoming him. The contraband was still there. The university stash now included a desk light, a roll of Ethernet cable, and a cheese grater. Mum had been busy. There was almost enough to fill an entire future.

After a couple of minutes Charlotte came back up the stairs.

'Derrick?'

He slammed the wardrobe door and fumbled the binoculars under Mum's bed. Then he stepped out to meet her in the hallway. She was leaning cautiously into his room, like she might find him doing something embarrassing she'd rather not see.

'Yeah.'

She jolted and cracked her elbow against the doorframe. 'Christ!' she said, pressing a hand to her elbow and rubbing it. 'Mum just phoned. She's been held up at work. You're making dinner.'

'Why me?'

'I'm too messed up to manage anything for myself, remember?'

Derrick shuffled his feet. His cooking would probably just mess her up more. 'I didn't think you ate dinner any more.'

She answered with a particularly unhelpful shrug.

'All right. Want to eat now?'

'You probably need it more than me.'

Derrick decided that it was as close to an agreement

as he was likely to get. She was in full-on indifference mode. At least it was better than the crying.

He went downstairs to the kitchen. If he could get dinner out of the way it would still leave him with plenty of time to go out later. There were still a few hours left until nightfall.

Derrick's cooking abilities extended about as far as opening a packet and sticking the contents in the oven. Even then he tended to burn it. Mum had once shown him how to do pasta. When he tried it himself the water had boiled over and practically melted his hands.

At least eating out of the dustbin was low-prep.

The oven whirred to life when he selected a temperature at random. A blast of cold hit him in the face as he opened the freezer. It was mostly empty – shopping hadn't been high on the list with everything that was going on – so he selected a half-empty box of fish fingers and some potato waffles. He tipped them out onto a black tray and shrugged. It seemed a fittingly depressing dinner.

Once it was in the oven, Derrick turned to stare out of the back window, where the Beast had stared in at him. Today he would put an end to it. With the Beast captured he'd regain control and start to make things better.

Impatience needled at him gently and he forced his legs to stop jittering.

The cat jumped suddenly onto the outside windowsill. Derrick reared back in surprise and clattered into the dining room table. Then he burst out laughing as she peered quizzically at him through the glass. It felt like the laughter had been bottled up for a long time. He sank to the floor and let it pulse out of him. Today would be the end of all the terrible things that had happened to him and his family. For the first time in months he could laugh without feeling ashamed.

'What's so funny?' Charlotte walked in.

Derrick swallowed and righted himself. He opened the back door for the cat, who wound herself around his ankles.

'I was just thinking that this dinner might be the last terrible thing to happen to us.'

Charlotte dropped into a chair. 'Yeah, because we won't survive it.' Derrick felt more laughter rear up inside him but he held it back. It didn't feel right to laugh in front of her. It would be like teasing her with an emotion she didn't possess.

'I'll get some plates ready,' he said. Then he bit his lip. 'I didn't mean . . .'

Charlotte slowly turned her eyes up at him. 'It was an accident.' Her voice was cold and flat.

The memory of the scattered debris cut off his words. The shard of bloodied plate on the table where they were about to eat.

'It doesn't matter,' he said.

Derrick opened up the cupboard. The only plates left were the chipped blue ones they hadn't used for years. He grinned at her. 'At least it won't happen again – there's barely anything left to smash.'

She rolled her eyes at him. He set a pair of plates on the table and then opened the cutlery drawer.

'You're cheerful,' said Charlotte as he clattered forks onto the table.

A sudden urge to run upstairs and check on the cage welled up inside him and he had to tell himself that it wasn't necessary. Nothing would happen until after dark, under the cover of night. That was when the allotments came to life.

'Why shouldn't I be?'

Charlotte shrugged. 'Because you live here.'

That made Derrick grin again. All of that was about to change.

The food seemed to glow orange when he dropped the scorching hot tray onto the table. Charlotte's nose wrinkled at the greasy offering.

'This dinner gives you no right to be cheerful,' she said, and forked a few bits onto her plate.

Derrick took what was left. It was a lot more than half.

'So . . .' said Derrick, as he watched her chew unenthusiastically on a limp fish finger. 'Good day?'

'Why would you ask me that?'

'I don't know. Better than being at school. At least your exams are over now.'

Charlotte considered this. Slowly, like a melting ice lolly, the fish finger speared on her fork broke in half and tumbled onto her plate. 'It's not over yet.'

'What do you mean?'

'I need to get the grades for university.'

Derrick stabbed at a potato waffle. 'You will though, right?'

'I bloody well better. I'm not staying here any longer than I need to.'

For some reason he thought of the knives and medication hidden away inside the wardrobe. She had already tried to drastically reduce her time here.

The waffle crumbled between his teeth. Flecks of processed potato hit the table when he spoke. 'It won't follow you.'

She raised an eyebrow at him.

'Your – you know – your sadness. It's like it's trapped us here. I'm going to make sure it doesn't stop you going to university. It'll be better then.'

Charlotte rested her chin on her hands. She looked at him for a long moment before she said, 'You promise?'

Derrick answered with a nod. It was true. It *had* to be true.

They ate in silence for a few minutes. The food was soggy in his mouth. He probably should have cooked it for twice as long. The slick taste of grease stuck in his throat.

He lowered his fork onto the plate. 'None of this is your fault.'

'Yeah, *I* know how to use the oven.'

'No, I mean, all your problems and whatever.'

Charlotte took a moment for the words to settle. She finished off a mouthful of waffle and nodded slowly. 'Thank you. It means a lot that you understand that.'

He *did* understand. Now that the cage was out there and waiting, it all made sense for the first time. This was how he would save them. After tonight he would puncture a hole in the bubble around the house, and the darkness would drain away. Everything would just be *normal*.

'I'm going to sort it out. Tonight.'

'What?'

Derrick couldn't hold it in any longer. He wanted her to know that everything was going to be all right. 'I wasn't going to tell you until it was over. Remember the news story about the panther?'

Charlotte nodded reluctantly. 'No one'll shut up about it.'

'Because it's out there! I've seen it! Everything that's gone wrong happened since the panther showed up. I didn't realise it before. That's why I couldn't control anything. It trapped us. I'm going to show it who's really in control.'

Charlotte looked at him as if he'd lost his marbles. She let out a long breath through her nose and rested her elbows on the table.

'I don't think you do understand.'

A jolt of pain in his stomach made him flinch. 'That's what you always think.'

'It's not your fault, Derrick. I just don't think you really *can* understand.'

Heat flooded his skin. The pain seemed to spread through his body and he had to grip the edges of the table. She was so selfish! All he wanted to do was save them and she *still* treated him like he was useless. The joints of his fingers crackled. He'd held his tongue for too long. He didn't care any more.

'I'm the only one trying to do anything about it!' He slammed the table with his fist. The plates and forks rattled. 'No one bothers to notice how much it's ruined my life! It's destroyed everything!'

He shoved his chair back so hard that it toppled over and smacked the kitchen floor. Charlotte just watched him like he was a kid having a tantrum, her hands flat on the table. Her indifference just made his anger hotter and hotter.

'There has to be a way to stop it!' he shouted. 'This is our best chance!'

He stormed past her and up the stairs. He didn't stop until he was face down on his bed, the door slammed hard behind him.

The thought crept into his brain before he even noticed it was there. Junk food. It was the only way he knew to take control.

You don't want it.

After he'd caught the Beast he wouldn't need it any more.

He grabbed the pills from their hiding place under his mattress. They weren't making any difference, but for some reason he felt like he had to keep trying. Charlotte had been on them long enough. He swallowed one down and shoved the box into his pocket. It wasn't exactly as satisfying as shovelling junk food into his body.

To distract himself he grabbed his laptop and opened it up to Facebook. Even though today had been the last day of school he had no notifications. That was hardly surprising. But he'd hoped that someone might have wished him a happy summer. Suggested that they meet up. But there was no one that would ask. He should just be happy that they'd stopped sending him abuse.

Instead he scrolled down his feed to read the messages people from school had sent each other. It was about as close as he'd ever get to being like them.

A single post halfway down his feed brought his scrolling to a sudden halt. He wrapped his arms around his stomach. It felt like knives were being shoved into his guts. The words didn't seem to make sense. It made his head swim. Yet he knew exactly what they meant.

It was a status update from Tamoor.

Today i am a MAN!!! Always the first!!

Derrick stared at the post as if he were deciphering a secret code. It could mean only one thing. When they used to hang around at the old warehouse they'd talk about girls. Tamoor had always said that he could never consider himself a man until a girl made him one.

The pain was almost too much to bear. It felt like the atmosphere in the house had finally become too heavy. Any second now it would crush him into paste. When he tried to breathe it was like a wet rag was draped over his face.

He clicked through to Tamoor's profile and hurried down to his timeline posts. It was full of new messages from guys at school. All the meatheads Tamoor had started hanging around with when he was finished with Derrick. They were posted just minutes after the status update.

Mate! How was it?!?!

No way, cuz! msg me!

Give her one for me!!

Every single word stabbed. He doubled forward, face pressed against the screen.

Derrick had always known that Tamoor would get there before him. That wasn't exactly a shock. But not with Hadley. She was the only girl in the world that Derrick wanted for himself. Tamoor knew that. He knew it!

Derrick stumbled to his feet. Anger gnawed at him. Thoughts of junk food twisted in his mind. He gripped the back of his chair so hard that his knuckles bleached to bone-white.

No. No more bingeing. He didn't need it. This was one final test. The depression was doing everything it could to make him give up. To keep him trapped here for ever. He wouldn't let it win. Tonight he would regain control, once and for all.

It wasn't quite dark outside yet, the sun was still sinking, but he had to take action. There was only one thing that would fix all of this.

It was time to go and catch the Beast.

Chapter Thirteen

The warehouse loomed up in front of him, a towering shadow in the half-light. Derrick stopped at the gap in the fence where the gate used to be. One hand rested on the rusted post.

Why are you here?

When he stepped out of the door Derrick had been thinking of nothing but the Beast, but rather than walking in the direction of the allotments entrance he had gone around the block to the other side.

The courtyard stretched away from the road. Scraggly weeds grew tall through cracks in the uneven tarmac. Derrick walked past the old air-conditioning unit where he and Tamoor used to lounge on hot days, as if the rusted metal boxes still worked. It was out here that he'd told Tamoor about the incident. It was right here that their friendship had come to an end.

The main door to the warehouse had always been locked. They used a thick metal bar they found nearby to prise it open. The air grew cooler as Derrick stepped inside. Only a few narrow beams of failing sunlight pierced through the darkness. There wasn't much to see inside, just the dusty concrete floor and a precarious climbing frame of scaffolding in the far corner. It had been stripped bare. Scraps of metal and wood lay here and there, and he accidentally kicked an old beer can. It clattered away and settled somewhere in the shadows. Derrick remembered how they'd sometimes come here to drink, when they could get hold of some.

The warehouse used to be a refuge. Now it felt like he was trespassing. It should be full of happy memories, but it felt like nothing more than a shell. It had been gutted. A part of him wanted to burn it to the ground.

It was on a night like this that he had confessed to Tamoor how he felt about Hadley. It probably hadn't been much of a surprise since Derrick used to talk about her pretty much constantly. He wasn't embarrassed about it, that wasn't why he'd not said anything before. It was more that he could never quite find the right words to explain it properly. It wasn't like it was just a stupid little crush. As things got worse at home Derrick realised how much he needed her, and this had always felt too personal to tell Tamoor, too important, and, he acknowledged now, too delusional as well.

Derrick kicked out at the metal wall. The heavy *boom* rung around the empty interior. He brimmed with anger, but he didn't really know who he was angry at.

A patch of bluish light cut out of the back wall gave away the other entrance. It was nothing more than a hole that must have been cut by whoever had to remove all the equipment when the place shut down. Derrick ducked through it, the ragged metal brushing his hair.

It led to a small space cut off by the allotment fence. A small outhouse beside the door hid the remains of a toilet inside. They used to use it, until it overflowed and began to stink.

Derrick looped back around the side of the warehouse, where the allotment fence boxed it in, as if it were trying to stop the warehouse from stealing any more of its land. Somewhere in the tangle of weeds that now grew over in the corner was concealed, he knew, a hole just big enough to crawl through. They'd used it when they were younger as an escape route, when they used to tear through the allotments with the neighbours yelling after them. Derrick couldn't spot it, the overgrowth was too dense. He probably wouldn't fit through it any more.

As he turned back onto the courtyard a burst of laughter came from over by the gate. Derrick looked up to see a group of four guys walking in off the pavement. It was too dark to make them out. He tried to duck back out of sight before it was too late.

'Who's that?'

Derrick recognised the voice. It was one of the meatheads from school, the first to reply to Tamoor's status update.

There was no point in trying to hide now. So he took a breath, tugged on the hem of his T-shirt, and stepped out of cover.

They were close enough for him to be able to make out their faces. The one who had spoken was nearest. His name was Grant, he was in the year above them. He had a big head without much hair on it. A thin moustache had grown on his top lip that didn't do much to compensate. It had been Grant who had recorded the video in the school toilet, after he'd snatched Tamoor's phone.

Two of the others were from Derrick's year. Despite matching their age, Derrick had managed to fall way behind them in the puberty race.

Lastly, half hidden behind the pack, stood Tamoor.

He brought them to your place.

'On the lookout for a new wanking spot, are you?' said Grant.

They all laughed in response. Even Tamoor. But he hung back, hands crammed deep into his pockets.

'I'm just going,' said Derrick, trying to step around them.

'Stand back, lads, he's coming!'

That achieved another laugh. Derrick tried to use the opportunity to get past them, but they spread out to block his way. Grant moved directly in front of him. At full height he seemed to tower over Derrick.

'You've not been in school,' he said.

Derrick tried to push down the fear crawling up inside him.

'That's very observant of you.'

Grant sneered. 'You know I can just punch you in your fat mouth, right?'

'Yeah, but that would just prove that you're more than indifferent to my existence.'

Grant's face screwed up in confusion.

Tamoor took the opportunity to peer in over his new mate's shoulder. 'Let him go, yeah. What does it matter?'

'You hear that?' said Grant. 'He's too pimp now to want anything to do with a little gay boy.'

Tamoor looked directly at Derrick for the first time.

'I've known that for a while,' said Derrick.

'You admit you're a gay boy, then?'

'Whatever.'

'Or maybe you're just crazy like your sister?'

Derrick stared at him open-mouthed. The one secret he'd thought that Tamoor would never tell. The one secret he'd thought was safe. He gritted his teeth. This betrayal hurt more than anything his old friend had done to him in the last three months.

'Get out of the way.'

Derrick shoved through them. He kept his eyes clear of Tamoor. A hand grabbed at his shoulder but he slapped it away.

'Just let him go, yeah?' Tamoor's voice, laced with anger.

Derrick didn't look back. When he reached the gate he turned onto the pavement. They shouted something after him. Derrick couldn't make out what, just the laughter that faded away behind him as he hurried down the road.

The pain in his stomach was so intense that it seemed to grip his legs. Every step became a struggle. But it was a fight he was determined to win. Nothing would stop him from getting to the allotments. It was the only thing he had left. When he found the Beast in the cage all of this bullshit would cease to exist.

It was dark now. He hurried around the block, back past his house and onto the allotment track. It was only when he reached the gate that he remembered he'd left the key in his room. He kicked out at the metal and watched it shake all the way along the alley. A dog started barking in one of the gardens. Derrick wedged his foot into the chain-link. He bit back the pain and heaved himself over the gate.

This time he didn't bother to look around for anyone who might see him. It didn't seem to matter now. It didn't seem possible that something could stop him.

The turmoil inside him didn't settle when his feet hit the grass. He headed straight past the oak tree and waded into the bushes. The cage was a dark square peeking up out of the leaves.

The door was shut.

Derrick stopped just a few paces from the cage. The sound of his heavy breathing filled the hush around him. It sounded like growling. It echoed in his head, made lead of his feet.

Slowly, he took a step closer. Then he lowered himself onto his knees and peeled away the camouflage of wood and branches. The smell of rancid meat filled his nostrils as he leaned forward to peer through the wire.

Nothing. The cage was empty. In the dim light that broke through the mesh he saw the steaks lying exactly as he'd left them. A hum of flies vibrated the air.

Derrick stared at the empty cage in disbelief. It couldn't be empty. It just couldn't. He wrapped his arms around himself as his insides writhed. Then he fumbled for his phone and swiped it to light it up. The flies scattered as he knocked against the wire and he spat one away from his lips.

The phone's light revealed nothing.

The cage door must have fallen closed by itself.

The stench of the meat, left to fester in the sun all day, clawed at his nose and throat. Derrick sat back on his haunches, tilted his head back and roared at the sky until he started coughing. Startled birds burst from the branches of the oak tree. He punched the cage, once, twice, again. Blunt pain throbbed from his knuckles up his arm. He pulled the box of Charlotte's pills from his pocket, scrunched it hard in his fist, and hurled it away into the weeds with as much force as he could muster.

The Beast wasn't there. He had failed. The trap would hold them away from the rest of the world until they were all destroyed, one way or another.

Derrick had failed to save his family.

A flash of intense pain doubled him over. A convulsion rippled through him and he tipped forward so that his head slammed into the wire. Goose pimples puckered across his skin as he tumbled sideways into the weeds.

He felt a bottomless hole open up inside.

Derrick only knew one way to fill it.

He fumbled the cage door open and reached to the back to grab a steak. The meat felt tough but slick, like a chunk of wet leather. Dark specks dropped onto the plastic floor. He felt his throat tighten. This was his punishment, and he had full control over it.

Before it made him choke again he sunk his teeth into the raw meat. His anger raged and he tore a chunk loose. His jaw ached as he chewed it madly. It refused to break apart. It was a few seconds before the taste registered on his tongue. It made him think of dead animals on the road, their innards strewn across the concrete. He swallowed the mouthful, jerking his head back to force it down his neck.

As soon as he took another bite his stomach convulsed. Heat swelled up inside his throat and he doubled over to vomit into the weeds. His insides felt like they would tear. It came from the very bottom of his gut. All the anger and resentment splashed thick and warm out of him.

When the heaving had ended, he spat his mouth as clear as he could manage. Then he fell sideways and rolled onto his back in the overgrowth.

He didn't cry. He forced himself not to cry.

Far above him a wreath of cloud scudded across the moon.

The Beast had escaped him, and he had no idea what was going to happen next.

Chapter Fourteen

In the mirror Derrick's belly looked less bulbous than usual. The skin sagged around the dividing fold like a deflated balloon. That was the only advantage of how sick he had been last night – the scale was a lot more forgiving this morning, the lightest he'd been in weeks.

He'd lain in the bushes for what must have been hours. For months he'd cast around for someone or something to blame for everything, but sprawled out in the darkness, covered in his own sick – there was no one else he could blame for that.

He breathed in and out to study how the shape of his stomach shifted in the mirror. There was nothing inside him. It was an emptiness he wouldn't be able to fill with junk food. Where there had been anger and guilt and resentment, now there was just hopelessness. Hopelessness and fear.

Derrick had no idea how to help his sister.

Maybe there was no way that he *could* help.

He showered quickly, trying not to look down at his body. When he was finished and dressed he stood in the gloom of the landing. Charlotte's bedroom door was shut tight. Downstairs the 24-hour news droned on. Derrick really didn't know what to do with himself now. There was still the whole summer holiday to get through. It almost felt pointless to keep trying.

He made his way to the garden. It was a cloudy day, but it didn't look as if it would rain. The bushes halfway down the fence looked less ragged than before. They seemed to have been smoothed back by the passing of time. The livid scratch marks were still visible through the remaining leaves, and although they had faded a little, the sight of them still made him shiver.

At the end of the garden he scraped open the gate. The scratches were still here too, the gatepost wearing them like proud scars. He ran his finger down the grooves absent-mindedly. A splinter nipped at his finger. Derrick flinched away and brought it automatically to his mouth. When he looked he found a sliver of wood caught beneath his skin.

'Brilliant.'

He kept sucking the finger and stepped out into the alley. The damp smell of rubbish greeted him. A phantom taste of rotten steak made him shiver, and he refocused his attention on the splinter settled under the skin deep enough that he couldn't pick it out with his teeth or nails. The splinter was like a second-place trophy in a two-man race. A sour little memento.

Derrick turned his eyes up to the chain-link. A lone figure was walking through the allotments. Whoever it was seemed unsure where they were going, tottering uncertainly on the narrow strips of grass between patches. He wondered if it was a tourist who had seen the panther on the news and come to gawk. It was only when the figure turned to face the fence that Derrick recognised him and saw that it was someone far worse.

Tamoor.

'Hey!' Derrick shouted.

Derrick jumped on the spot and waved his arms. His loose flesh shifted like cement turning in a mixer. Tamoor turned towards him and narrowed his eyes to try and locate the source of the noise. He'd always had terrible eyesight. Derrick wondered if his new mates knew about his glasses.

'Hey!' Derrick shouted again. He was at the fence, so he wove his fingers through the chain-link and shook it hard. The sight of Tamoor in *his* allotments made his blood boil. It wasn't right. It was the only place left that Derrick could go. If Tamoor was there, the darkness would find it and swallow it up.

Tamoor spotted him and began to make his way over. Derrick gripped the fence so hard that his fingers ached. His knuckles were nothing but scabs where he'd punched the cage.

'All right, Derrick?' said Tamoor when he reached the fence. 'Like old times, yeah?'

'What are you doing here?'

Tamoor looked back across the allotments and scratched the back of his head. He looked as if he were embarrassed to be there. Embarrassed to have been caught.

'I thought I'd just come and have a look for, you know . . .'

Derrick shook the fence hard. 'For what?'

141

'Your stupid panther!' shouted Tamoor, pushing his face close to the chain-link. 'That's what you were out looking for last night, yeah?'

Derrick stared at him like he hadn't made any sense. It had been over a week since he'd asked for Tamoor's help to find the Beast. Typical he'd decide to look for it now, after Derrick had failed.

Tamoor took a breath to calm himself down. 'It seemed important to you, you know? I'm sorry about –'

Derrick cut him off. 'Get out.'

'Huh?'

'I want you to get out of the allotments.'

'You think I want to be here? I remember what it did to you last time, thought I'd try and save you the trouble.'

Derrick pushed his face hard into the chain-link and stared Tamoor in the eye. 'Stay away from here. Yeah?'

A shadow of anger passed over Tamoor's face. If anyone talked to him like that he'd usually make them pay for it, but he just looked Derrick up and down, kissed his teeth, and stomped away towards the gate.

The allotments fell quiet. For a long time Derrick stood at the fence. Tamoor being there had made him angrier than he'd been in weeks. The allotments felt like *his* turf now. It still felt important. He shared it with the Beast. It had to still be here. Somehow Derrick knew that it wasn't finished with him yet.

It began to rain. A few light drops quickly grew into a steady downpour.

Derrick pushed open the back gate, and there was a sharp twinge of pain in his finger.

'Bloody splinter,' he said.

He examined his finger closely. Odd . . . He wiped his hand on his jogging bottoms and looked again. The skin was clean and unmarked.

The rain beat down on him hard. He turned to the gatepost. Where the scratch marks had been there was nothing but soaking wood. Derrick ran his hands up and down it, thinking the darkness of the wood saturated by rain was concealing them. Dirt smeared his fingers – but he couldn't feel a single notch.

He ran halfway up the garden, his T-shirt sticking tight to his skin. The bushes sprayed him as he shoved through them to reach the fence. No scratch marks here either, no matter how hard he looked.

You can't see them because of the rain.

Derrick ran for the house before he could wonder if that was true.

Chapter Fifteen

A few hours of searching for diet advice on the Internet was like being bludgeoned to death by all of his insecurities. Apparently the key to success was easy: make sure to eat five meals a day; only eat breakfast; never eat carbs; stay away from fruit; put gel in your hair; shave your head; bulk up your shoulders; wear skinny jeans; grow a bigger penis in five easy steps.

If he managed to do even half of it, he'd be either an entirely different person or dead.

Maybe neither outcome would be so bad.

When he couldn't take any more Internet advice he sat at his desk and stared at his fingertip. The splinter must have fallen out when he closed the gate. For some reason the thought of it made him shiver. It had stopped raining outside. He knew he should go and check for the scratch marks, but thinking about it made his chest feel tight.

Most of the afternoon was already over. Last night Derrick had failed to look after his family. He felt a sudden urge to phone his dad. They hadn't spoken ever since that conversation in the car outside. Derrick didn't really want to talk about it, but it would be good to get out of the house for a few hours, even if it wasn't a real escape.

The dial tone repeated until the answerphone kicked in. *You've reached . . .* Derrick hung up. His phone vibrated in his hand at the same moment. He looked at the cracked screen. It was a text from Hadley.

Hey Derrick. How r u? Doing anything right now?xx

The '*xx*' made his heart thump against his ribs. Usually she only left a single kiss. He could have debated with himself for hours whether the extra one meant anything, but he needed to act quickly. It sounded like she wanted to see him. If he took too long to reply she might change her mind.

Just when he'd given up on her . . .

Hey Hadley, I'm good. You? he tapped out, trying to sound as casual as possible. *Not doing much. Why you ask? x*

He sent it before he could think too much about it.

It was a pretty solid reply. It answered her question. It asked a question back, which gave her a reason to reply. Did it make him sound too eager? He swallowed hard and stared at the phone on his desk.

Her reply came through almost immediately. *Fancy McDonalds?x*

Only one kiss this time.

Derrick stared at the message. It didn't quite add up. He had lost Hadley – he had lost everything – when he'd failed to catch the Beast.

Yeah, he replied. *I'll head over now.*

145

Every pore on his body immediately began to ooze sweat. This was a turn of events for which he was severely underprepared. He breathed against his hand to check if he still smelled of sick but he couldn't tell. Quickly, he stripped off his T-shirt and sprayed a long cold squirt of deodorant into each armpit. Then he selected a new T-shirt (black XXL that usually made him look a little less like a hideous blob). The Internet had told him that black was slimming.

He hurried downstairs and slipped on his shoes as quietly as he could. It would be easier not to tell anyone where he was going. When he straightened up he tugged at his T-shirt, trying to arrange it into a flattering position across his stomach. He checked his reflection in the hallway mirror.

Good luck. You're going to need it.

His phone buzzed in his pocket as he opened the front door.

Meet u there x

Derrick frowned. He clicked the door shut behind him. Hadley only lived around the corner. Maybe she'd been out shopping or something. He turned onto the road and shook the worry out of his head. It didn't matter now. Anything had to be better than last night. Two sets of thoughts collided in his brain as he pounded along the pavement.

Don't get your hopes up, said one side.

She definitely loves you, insisted the other.

Maybe she'd finally seen sense and ditched Tamoor. Maybe she'd ditched Tamoor for *him*. Would that count as seeing sense? It was from his point of view. To literally everyone else it would probably look like madness.

Don't get your hopes up. It had been his mantra for a long time now and he trusted it. After last night, nothing good – like him and Hadley – could possibly happen. The darkness was too powerful to let that happen.

Still, the other side of his brain refused to shut up.

McDonald's was sandwiched between a discount fashion store and a newsagent's. Racks decorated the pavement with knock-off jeans and cheap T-shirts branded with roaring panther heads. It was just across the road from Hadley's dad's butcher's shop. They used to come here a lot, but it must have been a couple of years now.

Derrick spotted her sitting inside already at a window table. She tapped at her phone, her face scrunched into a frown. She only noticed him once he was inside and had approached the table. The frown broke into a smile, but it was obvious that it cost her some effort. It was the same practised smile he recognised from so many of her Facebook photos.

Hadley stood up and shoved her phone into her jeans pocket. For just a second Derrick thought she was going in for a hug. He leaned forward to meet it.

'Should we get food?' she said brightly, leaning away from him and turning towards the counter.

Derrick rocked backwards so quickly on his heels that he almost lost his balance. 'All right.'

Hadley had arranged her hair into a razor-sharp fringe that rested just above her eyebrows. The studs in her lip were a deep, dark black. Derrick walked behind her and forced himself not to look any further down her body than the back of her head, where a ponytail bobbed.

This close to dinnertime on a Saturday the queues stretched halfway to the door. Hadley joined the back of one, behind a pair of kids. When he went to join her she nodded for him to join a different queue, behind a middle-aged guy talking loudly on his phone. Between the noise of conversation, the sizzle of the fryers, and the bustle of the kitchen, there wasn't exactly much chance for them to talk to each other. Derrick kept trying to catch her eye, but she stared determinedly towards the front of the queue.

Luckily they moved quickly. They reached the counter at the same time. Derrick glanced across and tried to listen in on how much food Hadley was ordering. The last thing he wanted to do was end up ordering twice what she did. That was hardly the best way to look attractive. He couldn't make out a single word, so he decided to play it safe and halved his usual order: only one burger, with medium fries and a drink. After some thought he decided not to add chicken nuggets.

'Do you remember the time we got served by that guy who was convinced we were brother and sister?' said Derrick as soon as they were back at the table.

Hadley peeled the greasy wrapper from her burger. 'Oh god, yeah! You played along with it for ages!'

Derrick grinned. It hadn't been the first time he'd imagined what his life would have been like if he lived with Hadley.

'How's your *real* sister?'

Derrick let his grin fade. 'I don't really know any more.'

Hadley nodded absently. 'I texted her sorry for the other day, you know? She didn't reply.'

Derrick opened up his burger and picked out the soggy discs of gherkins. He pieced it back together and wrapped his jaw around it. For a split second the taste of meat flooded his mouth with the memory of the rancid steak, the way it stuck like sinew in his teeth, the flies buzzing against his face. His stomach groaned, but he forced himself to fight through it and kept chewing.

'I thought I understood,' said Derrick. 'But I don't.'

'Let's be honest,' said Hadley, brandishing a chip. 'She's a bit of a drama queen.'

The chewed glob of burger fell into the black hole of his stomach. It didn't seem to touch the sides. It made no impact on the emptiness that gaped inside him.

'It's more than that,' he said. He abandoned the food on his tray. 'I thought I had a way to fix everything. I was going to catch this stupid panther that's been hanging around here. The one in the newspaper?'

As the words came out he heard how stupid it sounded. He'd known all along, really, but it had felt so important. It *still* felt important.

'I thought that it would fix all our problems. I thought . . . I don't know. I just wanted to be able to do something.'

He felt his cheeks start to burn as he fell silent. Across the table Hadley dabbed at the corner of her mouth with a napkin.

149

After a moment she said, 'It isn't your job to do anything, you know.'

Derrick just looked across at her.

'Remember, I was the only friend she told after it, you know, happened? It was a lot of pressure. I felt so guilty because I didn't know what to do.'

Derrick still couldn't quite find any words. It had never really occurred to him that it affected anyone outside of his family. Not *really*. Everyone else had always seemed immune to it. Maybe it had spread even further than he realised.

Hadley twirled a chip at the edge of her mouth. 'I was surprised Tamoor knew about it. You guys were pretty close?'

Her tone of voice was innocent, but her eyes stayed trained on him, waiting for his reaction. She knew better than that. She knew that he and Tamoor were best friends for years before all this happened.

It made him so angry to think of Tamoor telling people about it – Hadley, the meatheads, and whoever else he'd blabbed to. He had always kept it a secret. Even when they stopped talking it had been the one piece of their friendship that remained intact, or so Derrick had thought.

'Yeah,' said Derrick. 'He knows.'

Hadley picked up her drink and pursed her lips around the straw. The black studs lurched towards each other. She looked sideways out of the window. The late summer light was turning a thick yellow. It seemed to weigh on the shops as they shut up for the day. Heavy metal shutters clattered hard against the pavement.

'I wanted to ask you about him, actually.'

Derrick expected a twinge of pain in his gut. He wasn't used to this unfeeling emptiness. It felt even worse than the pain had been – at least pain reminded him that there was still a chance he could make everything right.

His eyes settled on the burger on his tray, a single bite missing from it. He wasn't exactly going to ask how the happy couple were getting on. Ask how you two crazy kids got together. He'd rather jam the gherkins up his arse.

'He's being a bit funny with me,' said Hadley carefully.

Derrick forced himself to nod. It was the only vaguely appropriate reaction he could manage.

'He hasn't texted me since . . .' She trailed off and left the rest of the sentence to his imagination. Derrick expected her to blush. But her eyes stayed right on him. 'Is that what he's like?'

Derrick shrugged. 'I don't think I ever really knew what he was like.'

'Did you see what he put on Facebook? I mean, honestly. And then he stands me up today.'

Derrick felt his heart grow as cold as his abandoned burger. 'You were supposed to see him today?'

'Yeah,' said Hadley, scrunching a napkin in her fist. 'We were supposed to meet here.'

Derrick turned to face the window.

You were second choice.

Across the road a shop owner piled bin bags onto the pavement.

You're only here because he isn't.

'I'm not really hungry any more,' he said, looking at his tray.

'Me neither, really.'

They combined the detritus on their trays and Derrick crammed it into the nearest bin. The sun was still warm on his skin when they headed out onto the street. He walked a few steps ahead of her to try and avoid conversation.

All she had wanted was some inside information on Tamoor, as if he'd know anything about him any more. Some part of his dumb brain just couldn't let go of the idea that she actually wanted to spend time with him. He was such an idiot to harbour any hope whatsoever. About anything.

Another thought occurred to him. Tamoor had been in the allotments looking for the Beast when he was supposed to be meeting Hadley. Derrick quickly shut down the whisper-voice encouraging him to root out a meaning in that fact. He told himself, firmly, that it did not mean anything at all.

They dodged the last of the day's shoppers and pushed through a group of younger teenagers who crowded off a bus. They only spoke again when they turned off the high street towards home.

'Anyway,' said Hadley. 'He just stuck it in and lay there.'

Derrick burst out laughing before he could stop himself. The unwanted image dropped into his mind like an Internet pop-up.

Hadley laughed with him. The sound of her seemed

to shrink the emptiness inside him. The good feeling lasted until they reached the corner that joined their roads.

'Thanks for meeting me. At least you're reliable, right?'

Just yesterday those words would have made his heart soar. Now he recognised that they were meaningless. Nothing she said to him mattered any more. There was nothing for him to decode, to agonise over for the rest of the night.

He stepped forward and pulled her into a hug. Her head pressed against his shoulder and he breathed in the scent of her hair. He held her like he might never see her again.

'Let me know if you see Tamoor,' she said, trying to pull away from him.

He clamped his thick arms around her back and pulled her tight to his stomach.

Hadley laughed uncomfortably. 'Ok, I'm going home now.'

She tried to squirm out of his grip but he held tight, only letting her get far enough away for there to be an inch between their faces. He could feel her breath against his skin. For just a second he thought about how he was so much stronger than her. How easy it was to capture her inside his hideous fat arms.

'Get off me!'

Hadley pulled backwards and he let her go. She toppled onto the pavement. Derrick moved to give her a hand up but she slapped it away.

'I'm sorry,' he said, trying to laugh, trying to make it a joke.

'What's wrong with you?' she said, already hurrying up the hill away from him.

For the first time in his life he didn't watch her go. He put his head down and aimed for home.

The sun had slipped down below the roofs. Vapour trails smudged across the sky in orange and pink streaks. They broke apart and evaporated in slow motion. He felt hollow. He stood and waited to feel something about what had just happened. Nothing came.

At least he knew the truth now. Maybe he'd finally be able to move on. Maybe things would start to get better for him. Damn it – hope again, wheedling in . . . he knew it would be crushed as soon as he got home.

He was already past the allotment track when he saw it. A jolt of horror raced through his body. Some kind of autopilot carried him numbly onward.

There was an ambulance parked outside his house.

Chapter Sixteen

The front door shut him into silence. Derrick stood in the middle of the hall. The blue lights from the ambulance crawled across the walls. The cat's eyes flashed where she sat, halfway up the stairs.

The lights glided quietly away from the house. No siren. Tracks of mud darkened the carpet and trailed up the stairs.

They were already carrying her down from her room when he'd got there. The green uniforms had talked over each other so that it was impossible to make out their words.

Charlotte had been conscious, a plastic breathing mask hanging loose from her face. As soon as she saw him she had started saying, 'It was an accident,' over and over again. Blood was coming from somewhere.

Mum followed them down the stairs. Her face was grey and stretched taut. She wasn't crying. It seemed like she should be crying.

The muddy footprints guided him upstairs, past the cat, to Charlotte's room. Derrick stood in the doorway. The light was still on. Her laptop screen glowed. Music softly interrupted the silence with a thin mechanical beat. The carpet was littered with jagged shards of pottery, pink and white and blue. The top of her dresser, where the ornaments used to be, was bare. The carpet was wet with dark red bloodstains. Near the dresser there was a thick wet patch. Fat droplets had sprayed out from it in random patterns, staining the walls, the bookshelf, the bed. Scrunched up on top of the sheet were an empty pillow case and a bundle of towels – all tainted. Derrick inhaled the metallic smell.

The paramedics hadn't said anything to him. Mum had barely seemed to notice him when he asked to go with them – it was as if she didn't even hear.

It was an accident. That's what Charlotte had said.

So much had changed, in so little time. He had only been away for an hour. It was as if time inside the house acted faster than it did outside. The darkness flexed around him. They must have been pulled further away from everyday reality than he'd realised.

The cat clung at his heels as he walked back downstairs. His whole body felt light. It was hard to breathe properly. The lights in the sitting room were off. Pinpoints of LED punctuated the darkness from the TV set, the flashing router, and the answering machine – Derrick absentmindedly pressed the play button on the latter. The robot voice told him that a message had arrived just minutes after he'd left the house to meet Hadley.

Hi, it's Dad, calling to return Derrick's call. Sorry I missed you earlier, I got held up. Hopefully we'll catch up soon. I, uh, phoned the house phone thinking I might catch Charlotte. But you must not be there. Lots of love.

A long bleep cut off the message. The machine died.

Derrick walked through to the kitchen and flicked on the light. The cold floor sent chills up through his bare feet. He had no memory of taking off his shoes and socks. He scraped a chair out and sat down at the table, leaned forward on his elbows.

Was this your fault?

Everything he had said to Charlotte the night before, right here at this table, tumbled headlong through his mind. He must have sounded crazy, babbling like an idiot about the panther. It had been so obvious to her that he didn't understand a single thing.

It must have made her feel so alone.

And he'd taken her pills. What if they might have stopped this?

The pit in his stomach felt like it was going to suck every worthless scrap of him down into nothingness – turn him inside out and make him disappear. Good riddance.

That's when he felt it. Guilt. For months it had weighed him down and he'd known it was there, the force of it. He had spent so much time dodging around it, not daring to feel anything more than he could bear. The junk food had helped with that. It had given him something easier to feel guilty about. Now though, it came to him full force, and he hated it. He hated himself.

He should have done more to help.

Derrick jumped to his feet. The chair clattered backwards to the floor. He threw open the kitchen cupboards and his eyes looked from shelf to shelf. Christ, how long had it been since anyone did any shopping? The cupboards were bare, occupied only by a few random tins, jars of pasta sauce, a bottle of ketchup. This was how bad things had become.

The light from the fridge washed out his skin. Inside was a tub of butter, a half-drained bottle of milk, more ketchup. The only real food was a plate of grey chicken wrapped in cellophane. The sight of it made him want to throw up.

The empty kitchen forced him to remind himself that junk food wouldn't solve anything or give him any control. Not really. His feelings were wired all wrong and they couldn't be trusted.

When the phone shrilled through the house, the cat pinned back her ears. The ringing sliced through Derrick too, but he stood over the ringing handset, not moving to silence it. Eventually the answering machine clicked in.

Derrick, it's Dad. His voice was strained, even through the layer of fuzz that hung on the line. Behind him came the snarl of traffic. *I've just heard. I'm on my way over to you before I go to the hospital. Are you ok? I'll be there soon.*

The blare of a car horn bled into the answering machine's *bleep* as the call cut off. Derrick walked back into the kitchen. He stood at the back door and let his reflection stare back at him in the glass. He pivoted to study the swell of his belly from different angles. It was filling up with the guilt, straining at the fleshy con-straints of his gut.

158

The cupboard doors still hung open. The empty shelves were like accusations. The heavy atmosphere of the house felt like it was pulling at the fabric of his body.

He needed to get out of the house.

He couldn't face seeing Dad. It would just make him feel even more useless.

He ran out into the garden. Cool air flooded his lungs. He hurried past the decking, and remembered seeing Charlotte the other night – cigarette smoke leaking from between her fingers.

You're acting like she's dead.

She might be.

He pictured her eyes flashing green like the panther's.

The cold grass itched between his bare toes. There was only one place that would give him any chance of escape. Twigs and stones dug into the soles of his feet as he wrenched open the back gate and stepped into the alley.

This is where everything that had happened in the last few weeks had started. The criss-cross shadows of the chain-link, the hot stink of the dustbins. Ever since he'd seen the Beast here, he felt as if his life had separated from everything that came before.

The allotments stretched out beyond the fence. He felt connected to reality here. He groped along the metal with his fingers and found the hole in the fence. The rough ground tore at his knees as he dropped down to wrench it as wide as it would go. He wriggled in, shoulders first. Sharp metal cut at his skin. The girth of his stomach folded over itself as he tried to force it through. Even when he breathed all the air out of his lungs his body would barely fit. He had to squirm like a beached whale until his legs popped clear.

The vegetable patches harboured their dark shapes in the night. Vines twisted around the wooden frames and above it all towered the oak tree, standing guard, the smaller trees crowding around as if for safety. Derrick breathed the musty air in deep. He wanted to save it inside him. The allotments carried on as usual. They grew and flourished. It was all wonderfully indifferent to his existence.

Derrick ran, leaves and dirt flying up at his feet.

Memories collided with him.

Three months ago: he had come home early from dinner at Hadley's house and found his sister, collapsed on her bedroom floor. She had slumped off her bed into a puddle of vomit. At first he'd just stood in the doorway and said her name, *Charlotte, Charlotte.*

Charlotte had been breathing. Empty pill packets were piled on her dresser but she must have brought most of them back up. The room had stunk of alcohol and bile.

The ambulance lady on the phone had asked him what she had taken and he had read the names off the packets. Then he'd sat and waited for the paramedics to arrive. Somewhere along the way he must have called Mum, because she was there too. She cried and wrung her hands but it was as if she were afraid to touch her own daughter. She must have known there was nothing she could do. All she could do was join in the chant, *Charlotte, Charlotte. What have you done? Charlotte.*

Derrick reached the edge of the bushes and skidded to a halt. There was nowhere left to run. He jumped into the overgrowth, and tried to spot the scrunched up packet of antidepressants he'd thrown away the other night. He had some vague idea that he would just put them back in the house, in Charlotte's room.

Derrick remembered sitting on the cracked concrete outside the warehouse in the days afterwards. He remembered every single word he'd said as he spilled it all to Tamoor.

She's crazy, man. She's gone batshit crazy.

Just then, something hit into his back so hard that it pitched him forward and down. His face hit the ground and dirt flew into his mouth. A sharp pain tore across his shoulders as something slashed his skin. Derrick tried to scream but the weight pressed him into the ground. His lungs were empty. The darkness wouldn't let him breathe.

The weight on top of him radiated heat. Wet, heavy breaths washed over his neck.

Derrick tried to struggle loose. As soon as he moved a growl rumbled right beside his ear. It vibrated through every fibre of his body. The thick smell of blood choked his nostrils.

A hunter never gives up.

The voice was like an earthquake. Derrick could feel a heartbeat pounding against his back. It seemed to calm the frantic hammering of his own heart until it slowed and fell into step.

He grows tough in the face of his enemies.

And then the pressure was gone. Derrick rolled over, breathing hard, gasping cool air.

The allotment was as empty as ever. Fear tingled on his skin but his heart remained calm. The branches of the oak tree seemed frozen mid-applause.

Chapter Seventeen

A key clicked in the front door. Derrick's eyes snapped open at the sound. He tried to force himself up from the sofa but his body wouldn't shift. The lights from the router flickered across his face. The cat jumped down from where she had spent the early hours of the morning curled against his stomach. Sweat soaked his T-shirt. He hadn't bothered to change after he stumbled home from the allotments.

'Derrick?'

Dad's voice. It was enough for Derrick to heave himself to his feet. He glanced at the time. It was already late morning. He didn't know what time he'd got back home, but his eyes felt heavy, like he hadn't slept for more than a few hours. As he walked into the hall he realised that the front of his T-shirt was still spattered with dirt.

Sunlight dazzled him through the open front door. Dad stood in the opening. The ghost of a smile broke across his unshaven jaw when he saw his son.

'So you *are* here.' He tried to sound bright, but his voice was thick with fatigue. 'Are you ok? You didn't answer when I came round last night.'

Derrick rubbed his eyes. 'Sorry. I . . . fell asleep or something. Is she here?'

Dad nodded. 'Your mum's bringing her in from the car. She's very tired, so . . .'

The sentence trailed off. Derrick completed it in his head. It was a warning not to say anything that might upset her. Not to stare too much. Not to mention the word *suicide*. It wasn't difficult to figure out. He'd negotiated her for long enough now.

The air in the hallway sat in his lungs like tar. The atmosphere was heavier than ever this morning. The breeze that drifted in through the front door seemed as if it were reaching him from another reality. Derrick could hear Mum murmuring softly and the sound of a slow footfall coming up the driveway.

They appeared in the doorway. Mum was leading Charlotte by the arm, as if she'd forgotten how to walk. Somehow his sister looked even skinnier than before. Her grey skin clung tight to her face like a mask. The spots around her neck glared an angry red. She rolled her bloodshot eyes as Mum fussed at her. An oversized coat was slung across her shoulders. It made her look like a child.

One of her forearms was bandaged from wrist to elbow.

Mum was wearing long sleeves. Her own bandage was hidden. Now they had matching wounds.

When Charlotte stepped over the doorjamb Mum clung to her arm as if the extra effort might make his sister fall. Charlotte flashed her a glare and tugged her arm free, stepping decisively into the hall.

'For God's sake,' she muttered.

Mum shut the door with a *thud*. Derrick felt the weight of the house settle around them. They all traipsed into the kitchen. The empty cupboards were still gaping and Derrick hurriedly shut them.

There was a long moment of silence. Everyone stared anywhere but at somebody else. Derrick tried to think of something to say, but he couldn't find a single word. He crammed his hands down deep inside his pockets.

Eventually Charlotte glanced up at Dad and slipped the coat from her shoulders. He took it from her and folded it over his arm. Charlotte flexed her bony shoulders and ran a shaky hand through her hair. Then she stared down at her shifting feet. If her skin wasn't such a stubborn grey Derrick was sure she'd be blushing.

It was impossible to think of what to say to someone who had almost killed herself. To someone who might not have been around to hear it.

It was an accident. That's what she'd said.

'It's been a long night,' said Mum. She stepped around Charlotte to drop her keys onto the table. 'You should get some sleep. We'll make up the sofa.'

It wasn't a suggestion. Charlotte huffed an exasperated breath but didn't argue. She seemed glad for an excuse to get away from them. She let Dad squeeze her shoulder gently, and then slid past them all into the hallway. Her good arm clung tightly to the doorframe.

As she slipped into the front room their eyes met for the first time since she'd stepped through the door.

Only for a moment. Derrick tried his best to arrange his face into some kind of apology. But she'd already turned away before he could manage it.

'I'll keep an eye on her,' said Dad.

When they were alone Mum untied her shoes and chucked them into a corner. Then she swaddled Derrick in a hug.

'Tell me what happened,' he said into her shoulder.

She sighed and let him step away from her. 'It really was an accident.'

A burst of relief welled up inside him. It was less than a second before the guilt swamped it. Whether it was an accident or not he should have been able to stop it. If he'd caught the Beast this wouldn't have happened at all.

'We were arguing, and she started throwing her ornaments against the wall. Somehow one of them sliced open her wrist.'

Derrick winced at the thought. Suddenly he remembered the blood spattered across her bedroom carpet. It must have been a serious cut.

'It wasn't the cut that frightened me,' said Mum. She looked at him intently and shook her head. 'It was that she didn't seem to care.'

That cast them back into silence. They could hear Charlotte and Dad talking quietly in the other room.

'You're filthy,' said Mum eventually, her eyes scanning the front of his T-shirt.

'I was in the garden,' he said quickly. He dislodged his T-shirt so that it hid the shape of his body underneath.

166

'I leave you alone for one night and you sleep outside?'

Derrick felt the claws across his back, the weight pinning him onto the grass. The back of his T-shirt must be completely shredded. There was no way he could make up an excuse for that. Hurriedly he pressed his back to the wall. He had not seen what attacked him – but it couldn't have been anything except for the Beast. Nothing else could have loosed that bone-chilling growl. That voice like an omen.

'Dad and Charlotte are talking again, then?'

Mum cracked a tired smile. 'He always did have great timing.'

Derrick glanced into the hall. 'I need to talk to her too.'

Mum frowned. 'She probably wants some time alone. The doctor said she needs to rest. Can you go upstairs and get a clean blanket and pillow?'

The stairs protested loudly under his weight. He moved quickly in the hope that they wouldn't notice the state of his T-shirt. The Beast had marked his back. He was its territory now.

The university stash spilled out of the wardrobe. He bundled it back inside and grabbed a fleece blanket from the top shelf. Before he returned downstairs he found himself inside Charlotte's doorway. The room was exactly as it had been last night. It still looked like a murder scene. She shouldn't have to find it this way. Derrick dropped to his knees and started scooping up broken pieces of ornamental figurine. He ferried them quickly to the bin. But there was nothing he could do about the blood.

'I'm pretty sure the carpet's ruined.'

Derrick whipped around to find Charlotte leaning against the doorframe. She nodded at the splinters of pink and blue cupped in his hands.

'Careful,' she said, stepping around him. 'You could get a nasty cut off those.'

'You're not supposed to be up here,' he said.

She slumped back onto her bed and shoved the pile of bloodied towels aside. The sight of it didn't seem to bother her. She had reverted to unfeeling mode. Her wrist could still be bleeding and she'd just shrug it off.

'They can't follow me everywhere. I said I needed the toilet.'

Derrick dropped the broken pottery into the bin and worked on cleaning up the rest. He tried to keep his hands away from the biggest of the blood spatters.

'Are you ok?' he said. It was a stupid question. But he couldn't think of anything else.

'Yeah, I'm ok.'

More shards of ornament pattered against the bottom of the bin. Charlotte's whole body sagged back on the bed like a half-empty sack of bones. When she breathed no part of her seemed to inflate. Derrick stayed on the floor.

'Mum wanted me to stay and look after the house,' he said. 'And the cat.'

'We all know how important the cat is.'

'I wanted to go to the hospital with you.'

'It doesn't matter.'

'I'm sorry.'

'I wouldn't have wanted you there anyway.'

Derrick stared past her to the window. The pale blue of the summer sky was tinged with the grey of pollution. Sunlight glinted off a passing car. There was so much he wanted to say, but he didn't know which words to use.

'I meant I'm sorry that this happened. And about the other night.'

Charlotte rubbed at her eyes and pinched the bridge of her nose. Her eyes remained closed. 'What are you on about?'

'I thought I understood.'

Slowly, Charlotte opened her eyes. They were fractured with red veins, like shattered marbles.

'This isn't your fault. You know that, right?'

The guilt inside told him otherwise. 'When we argued the other night –'

A smile tugged at the edges of her mouth, but her eyes didn't follow suit. 'That wasn't why this happened.'

'I know. I mean, I think I know.' He shifted himself onto his feet to relieve the pain in his knees. 'I understand that I don't understand. I don't know how it feels. Because it's a real thing.'

Charlotte nodded. She opened her mouth to speak but Derrick talked over her. He didn't want his words to dry up.

'I feel angry,' he said, knowing that it was true. 'Because I can't do anything to make it better.'

Charlotte nodded again. 'I feel angry too. Because I'm not weak, Derrick. I'm *not*.'

Silence fell between them. A car glided past outside

the window. They each stared at different spaces on the wall. Eventually Derrick summoned the courage to reach into his pocket. He pulled out a soggy scrunched-up box of tablets.

'I took these,' he said, dropping them onto the dresser.

Charlotte almost looked amused. 'I know.'

'I thought you wouldn't need them if I could . . .' He trailed off, trying to work out her reaction. 'Would they have stopped this from happening?'

Charlotte tried her best to smile. 'It was an accident, remember? Anyway, that wasn't my only box.'

Derrick nodded. Although the guilt still sloshed around his insides, he felt relief too. Relief that he had told the truth. Relief that she wasn't screaming at him for it.

She pointed at the ruined box. 'Those tablets can cause erectile dysfunction, you know.'

'At least that's one thing you don't have to worry about.'

She flashed him the ghost of a smile. Derrick backed towards the landing.

'Are we supposed to hug or something?' he said.

Charlotte sniffed hard and wiped a hand under her nose. 'Not going to happen.'

Both of them managed to laugh. It sounded hollow. A fake and robotic noise that the house seemed to swallow up and cut short.

The words bubbled up out of him suddenly. 'You're not going to do it again, are you?'

Charlotte shook her head. 'No. I promise.'

Derrick nodded and turned towards the doorway. 'Ok. Now do what Mum says and go downstairs to sleep.'

She sighed, and shoved past him to the stairs. As soon as she was gone a deep breath made his lungs ache. It took a minute for him to gather the strength to step across to the bathroom. One hand was on the door when Mum stepped out of her room.

'It's rude to eavesdrop, you know.'

'And yet I do it anyway,' said Mum. 'I wanted to hear what you had to say. She's right, you know. You're not responsible for this. But sometimes you don't make it easy, either.'

Derrick nodded. He had tried to make it easier. The opportunity to stop all this from happening had been right in front of him, and he'd messed it up. So he *was* responsible, it didn't matter what they said.

'That promise she just made,' said Mum, lowering her voice. 'You have to remember that she's still . . . fragile.'

Derrick felt a lump lodge itself in his throat. When he spoke he half expected it to come out as a sob. 'You said it was an accident.'

'I think it was.'

'You think she'll do it again?'

'I don't know,' said Mum. She shook her head wearily.

Derrick swallowed hard. His eyes began to burn. Before she could say anything else he pushed through into the bathroom and locked the door behind him.

The mirrored doors of the medicine cabinet split his

reflection in two. He stared into his own eyes. Why did she want to hurt herself? She'd told him that she wanted to go to university. She thought she might be able to escape it there. Hurting herself again would just mean that she wouldn't be able to go. She kept making all these decisions that were bad for her.

That's the point, you idiot, his reflection spat back at him. *There isn't a reason. That's the whole problem.*

Derrick double-checked that the door was locked and then stripped off his muddy T-shirt. He fumbled his hands inside the material and stretched it taut between his arms.

No slash marks. No bloodstains.

It didn't make any sense. He could still feel the hot slash of the Beast's claws as they raked his skin.

Derrick threw the T-shirt to the floor and turned his back to the bigger bathroom mirror. His neck ached as he strained to see over his shoulder.

The skin was unblemished.

Derrick stared hard at his reflection, as if the wounds might open up before his eyes. This couldn't be possible. There was not a single mark on him.

Chapter Eighteen

One final desperate tug made Derrick lose his balance. He stumbled sideways into the cubicle wall. A flailing hand snagged onto a metal hook and he used the leverage to slide his weight down the wall until his butt hit the wooden bench.

'Everything ok?' said Mum through the curtain.

Derrick kicked the designer jeans off. 'No good.'

He heard Mum huff. Then the curtain was wrenched back and she pushed through.

'Mum!' Derrick cupped his hands over his crotch and tried to position his arms over his stomach. He couldn't decide which he was more ashamed of her seeing.

'It's nothing I haven't seen before,' said Mum as she retrieved the jeans from the floor. 'Now put your feet through these.'

She held the jeans open. Derrick sighed. He knew they wouldn't fit. They'd barely made it beyond his thighs. It had been like trying to dress a pair of doner kebabs. Shame made him want to kick them out of her hands. The last thing he wanted was a pair of expensive jeans. He never wore the cheap pair that he already owned. They were too uncomfortable now. An elastic waist was his chosen way of life, but Mum had insisted. It had seemed strangely important to her.

Mum lifted the jeans and tugged them hard up his legs. Derrick sucked in his belly, as if that would somehow make a difference. He hadn't yet found a way to suck in his thighs. The denim squeezed tight to his skin almost immediately above the knees. Mum tried to jerk them up but they wouldn't budge.

'How much can I pay you to stop?'

After one final tug Mum let go. 'Put your joggers back on.'

She left him to get dressed. His black jogging bottoms went up without a hitch and they felt more comfortable than ever before, but Derrick couldn't quite ignore the ember of shame that smouldered in his gut.

Before he left the changing room he checked himself from all angles in the mirror. The sight of his bulk made him want to smash his face into the glass. This really wasn't his chosen *anything*. It was just a reminder of how completely he had lost control.

He shoved the curtain aside and went out into the shop. The raised voices reached him immediately. One of them sounded all too familiar.

'How can you not have any bigger sizes?' Mum shouted as she brandished the pair of jeans at the shop assistant.

'I'm sorry, they're the biggest we do.' The assistant was a young girl, maybe Hadley's age, her eyes wide in an expression that closely resembled terror.

174

Derrick hurried over. 'It doesn't matter, Mum. Let's go.'

'It does matter!' shouted Mum. She threw the jeans at the assistant's feet. 'It's one simple thing and you're saying I can't do it!'

The shop was nearly empty. The only other customers were a couple who stopped what they were doing to stare. A shopping centre security guard swaggered his way over.

The assistant's voice quivered. 'I'm sorry . . .'

The security guard reached them. 'Is there a problem?'

'No, no problem!' said Derrick. 'We're going.'

He tugged hard on Mum's arm and steered her out of the shop. The security guard followed after them with a hand on his belt, as if he liked to pretend that he carried a gun. He only left them alone once they were well clear of the shop.

'Let's get something to eat,' said Derrick, before he remembered the tightness of the jeans. Mum just nodded, so he manoeuvred her towards the food court.

A worrying trend had overtaken the shopping centre. Every shop seemed to have found a flimsy excuse to sell panther memorabilia. The card shop had loaded baskets full with fluffy black panther toys. A few shops had stocked a DVD of a horror film called *Monster Killer Cat* (which boasted a giant CG tiger on its cover). The costume shops had dressed their mannequins in Black Panther uniforms.

It all made him feel irrationally angry. The Beast wasn't a toy. It wasn't an Internet meme. To Derrick, the Beast felt like *everything*.

They hurried past it all until they reached the cluster of tables and chairs ringed by fast-food outlets. Even though it was the school holidays it wasn't too busy. A few tables were occupied with families talking loudly over their assorted greasy meals. Derrick dropped Mum into a seat and cleared the table of a tray of half-eaten pizza. The tabletop was sticky.

Mum arranged her shopping bags around her feet. The trip was meant to be for him, but every shop they passed reminded Mum of something else she needed to buy for Charlotte. Today she'd bought a shower curtain. It was like she was just buying things for the sake of it now.

'What do you want to eat?'

Mum pulled a bottle of water from her handbag. 'I'm not really very hungry.'

Derrick let out a sigh. After what had happened with the jeans he didn't feel like eating ever again. He put his hands in his lap to keep them away from the table surface.

'I'm sorry for back there,' said Mum.

'Don't worry. It's only jeans.'

Mum rubbed her eyes so vigorously it was as if she were trying to pop them out of her head. 'I didn't mean to lose my temper like that. I just wanted to do something special for you.'

'Do you know what's really special? An iPad.'

Mum smirked at him. 'Don't push it. It was supposed to be a rite of passage. Your first designer jeans, you know? I wanted to try and make up for everything that's happened.'

Derrick stared across the table at her. He had been so wrapped up with the Beast that he had never considered that she might feel the same as he did. That she might blame herself for what Charlotte was going through. It would be easy to convince herself that it was deficient parenting. Maybe she felt guilty for his sake as well. That would explain the stupid jeans.

'It doesn't matter. It's not your fault.'

He reached out to her across the table and tried to ignore how it stuck to his skin. It wasn't Mum's fault. It was the depression's fault. It was the Beast's fault.

It was starting to feel most like his fault.

She took his hand and tried to smile at him. Her face seemed too tired to quite manage it.

'I'm going to put the knives back in the kitchen,' she said.

Derrick let go of her hand. 'What?'

'It's ridiculous to hide them. She knows where they are.'

'No, Mum.'

Mum lifted an eyebrow. 'We have to show her that we trust her. She'll be leaving home soon. It's time that she learned to make the right decisions for herself.'

Derrick stared at her. It didn't make any sense. Charlotte *never* knew how to make the right decisions for herself, and the depression getting stronger and stronger would only push her towards hurting herself. They were so close to getting her away to university. Mum was going to scupper them at the last moment.

He didn't want to argue. Not after she'd lost it with the shop assistant. Mum's face was so pale he could almost see through her. Tiredness seemed to be eroding her.

'Anyway, I need the space in the wardrobe for her uni stuff,' said Mum.

'I don't think it's a good idea,' Derrick said with as much finality as he could summon.

They sat in silence for a minute. Derrick felt the void stretch wide inside him. The feeling of shame was still there. It was strange. The jeans hadn't bothered him *that* much.

Mum reached into her handbag and pulled out a tattered square of paper. She flattened it on the table between them. It was a list, most of the entries scribbled out.

'There's still a few things I need to get for your sister. Not long to go now. Do you think they're getting on ok?'

Dad had volunteered to stay with Charlotte while they went shopping. In fact he had jumped at the opportunity. It was the first time in ages it had been just the two of them. He had turned up with DVDs, ice cream, and a couple of board games, like it was a sleepover. They were probably in the middle of strangling each other at that very moment. Still, Derrick felt better knowing that Dad was there.

'Did you and Dad break up because he has depression?' The question was past his lips before he even knew he'd been thinking of it.

Mum's eyebrows furrowed. 'Of course not. I'm offended you would think that of me. It's never as simple as that.'

'Sorry. He just –'

'I don't know what he told you.' Her face softened. 'It didn't make things easy for me. It would get bad and he didn't know how to deal with it. I probably shouldn't tell you this.'

Derrick leaned eagerly across the table and put his elbows in the sticky patch. He wanted to know it all. Even after all that had happened, it still felt like he knew barely a thing.

Mum sighed. 'Years ago I came home from work and found him passed out drunk. That was during those few months after the office made him redundant. When I managed to wake him up he got angry, and he told me he'd taken an overdose. I almost called an ambulance but then he started to cry and said it wasn't true. I went spare.'

Mum leaned back in her seat and ran her hand through her hair. 'You and Charlotte were both in the house. You didn't seem to have even noticed, but I'm sure Charlotte remembers.'

Derrick tried to remember. He fumbled in every corner of his mind but nothing connected. It seemed impossible.

'I don't want you to think any less of him,' said Mum. 'It was a difficult time.'

If he had forgotten – or, even worse, not *noticed* – something that big, so many other things could have passed him by. Mum was worried about letting him down; but it could easily be the other way around.

'I'm just so tired,' said Mum, pressing the palms of her hands into her eyes.

Derrick felt sick. The depression had not just torn them apart as a team, it had hit them all individually too. It had made them all give up. Charlotte had hurt herself. Dad had left. Mum was clinging on by a thread. And now he had let it defeat him as well.

He remembered what the Beast had said to him. *A hunter never gives up.* The thought extinguished the shame inside him.

He couldn't just give up like everybody else had. There was no one left but him. If he gave up he would be abandoning his family. He had to fight back, even if it seemed impossible. He would start tonight.

He grows tough in the face of his enemies.

'Let's go home,' he said.

Mum nodded, and they traipsed away from the food court towards the car park. As they passed a card shop Mum pointed at a basket brimming with fluffy panther toys.

'Do you think Charlotte would like one?'

Derrick looked at her and firmly shook his head.

Chapter Nineteen

The sight of the red meat glistening in the sunlight made bile rise into his throat. Derrick tried to keep his eyes away from it as he entered the butcher's shop. He fixed his gaze on the blank space of the back wall and tried not to retch. Both hands squeezed the edge of the counter. From somewhere in the back of the shop a toilet flushed.

The knives had gone back into the kitchen this morning.

Derrick had tried to argue, but Mum was firm.

He could barely control his anger. It was a mistake, he knew it. He imagined the darkness tunnelling into Charlotte's brain, like worms through an apple. Making her sleepwalk into the kitchen, her hands sliding open a drawer and finding the cold steel . . .

'She'll find a way, whatever we do,' said Mum as she slammed the cutlery drawer shut. 'We have to show that we trust her to make the right decision.'

Charlotte might think the right decision was to try again. She might not even be capable of making the decision for herself any more. Derrick had wanted to snatch them all up and run out into the garden. Bury them deep in the allotments.

The glass counter steamed over with his breath. His fidgeting hands smeared it with fingerprints. Restlessness had wheedled its way into his limbs. It was the same feeling as when he wanted to binge-eat, but now he was in control of it. *Really* in control of it: he felt restless because he had a plan that really could help them escape. He was desperate to set it rolling. First the butcher's shop. Then he would text Tamoor.

From the back of the shop a door creaked open. He heard water splash into the bottom of a sink.

'All right, Derrick,' said Hadley's dad as he dried his hands on a dirty towel.

He threw the towel behind him and tied an apron around the bulge of his stomach.

'What can I do you for?'

Derrick clenched his fists on top of the counter. 'I need two bags of blood.'

'This is still the stupidest thing you've ever done.'

Tamoor stepped through the allotment gate. Derrick resealed it after him with the padlock and slipped the key down into his pocket. He didn't feel so comfortable here any more, as he once had. The allotments refused to offer up their secret to him. This might be his last chance.

'It's here,' Derrick said. 'I saw it. The least you can do is help me find it.'

It had been easier to get Tamoor here than he had

expected. The two-line text message, the first to his former best friend in months, had taken half an hour to compose.

Thank you for looking for the panther the other day.

You're the only person who can help me catch it.

Crucially, it made Tamoor sound important, hinting at their previous expedition three months ago.

While he had been tapping it out he'd received a text from Hadley: *Is Charlotte ok?*

Derrick didn't bother to reply.

A strong breeze crackled through a loosely tied tarpaulin by a group of sheds. The leaves chattered high in the oak tree.

'I still don't get why you think this'll be any different to last time,' said Tamoor.

Derrick hid a smile and led the way through the vegetable patches. The rucksack bounced on his back.

Tonight he would prove that the Beast was *real*.

Tamoor followed behind. The whole way over to the allotments he'd been checking around, no doubt terrified in case anyone saw them together.

'So you hang out here now, then?'

'Not much choice now your new mates have taken over the warehouse.'

'You shouldn't have been there, you know. I helped you get away.'

They stopped underneath the oak tree. Derrick swung the rucksack off his shoulder and lowered it gently to the grass. He looked over at one of the smaller trees that grew just next to the oak. Metal glinted from one of its lowest branches.

'How big do you think this thing is, anyway?' said Tamoor.

'Big.' Derrick shivered as he remembered its breath on his neck, its heartbeat against his skin.

'We looked for a week and a half before and didn't see nothing.'

Derrick ignored him. The allotments seemed to be empty. Clouds rushed by overhead. It all seemed darker than usual and a chill in the air made goose pimples prickle across his arms.

'If it's bigger than you, we're screwed,' said Tamoor. He gobbed into the grass.

'Thanks for that.' He wouldn't let his anger take control of him. Not yet. Last time they'd been here together they'd argued worse than ever before. Derrick had thought it was over then, but it wasn't. Not until he said so.

He pointed at Tamoor's feet. 'There's dog crap there.'

'Ugh!' Tamoor jumped away from the base of the oak. His back knocked against the smaller tree. He lifted an arm to lean his weight on the low-hanging branch. 'Listen. I heard about your sister.'

Derrick kept control of himself. 'What you heard probably isn't true.'

'She tried to top herself again, yeah?'

'Is that what Hadley told you?'

Tamoor glanced away and kissed his teeth. It sounded like someone sucking a lemon. Derrick took the opportunity to step closer.

'I was sorry when I heard. Serious. And I'm sorry about the other day.'

'Thanks,' said Derrick drily. Then he deliberately turned to look at Tamoor's hand on the tree branch. 'Don't move.'

'Huh?'

'There's a *massive* bug on your hand.'

Tamoor's eyes went wide. 'Serious?'

Derrick nodded and reached slowly for Tamoor's hand. Tamoor shut his eyes tight as if he were expecting a fatal bite at any second. Derrick had to hold back a laugh. He should have started filming sooner.

'Get it off, yeah?'

With one hand Derrick wrapped his fingers around Tamoor's wrist to hold it in place against the branch. With the other he reached for the handcuffs that were already locked tight in place around the wood. The dangling end was open and in one swift move he closed it around Tamoor's wrist like a bracelet and clicked it tight.

'There,' he said, like an artist putting the finishing touches to a masterpiece.

Derrick stepped away and quickly calculated Tamoor's range.

It took a moment for his captive to realise what had happened. Tamoor opened his eyes a crack and peeked reluctantly down at his arm, as if the bug might make a charge for his face. He tried to pull his hand away but the chain snapped taut.

'What you doing?' Confusion muffled the anger in his voice.

Derrick didn't answer. He reached for his rucksack and unzipped it.

'Have you gone mental or something?'

'That's what you said about my sister.'

The cuffs clacked against the wood as Tamoor tried to shake free. Leaves showered over them.

The plastic blood bags were cool against Derrick's fingers, one in each hand. The thick liquid folded as he took them out of the rucksack, black as night in the darkness. The stains on Charlotte's carpet flashed across his mind. He laid them beside each other on the grass like a pair of lungs. The cloying redness swilled. It stained the inside of the clear plastic.

'What's that?'

'What does it look like?'

Tamoor swallowed hard. 'Blood.'

Derrick nodded and indulged himself with a smile. 'I thought the smell of your hair gel might put it off.'

'What the fuck you talking about?'

Derrick straightened up with one of the bags cradled in the crook of his arm. 'Ever heard of live bait?'

Derrick used the allotment key to puncture the top of the bag. The metallic pinch of the blood hit his nostrils immediately.

'You're crazy.'

'There's that word again.'

Derrick reached into his pocket and retrieved his phone. The camera was already up when he swiped the cracked screen. He wanted a record of his victory. The Beast wanted blood, so he would give it blood.

He would grow tough in the face of his enemies, if that's what it took.

Tamoor had abandoned him to the darkness when

he ruined their friendship; he had abandoned Hadley, when he stood her up the other day; and so now Derrick would abandon Tamoor to the Beast. The perfect sacrifice.

With the panther captured on camera he could put the footage online and expose it to the world. The Beast would lose its freedom, return it to his family.

Derrick stepped closer but stayed just out of range of Tamoor's free hand. Tamoor tried to pull away but the branch behind him blocked a retreat. The wood creaked and rattled.

'Is this about Hadley? Because you fancy her still?'

'Didn't stop you, did it?'

Tamoor couldn't keep the smirk off his face. 'I'm sorry, man, but come on. Really?'

Derrick smirked back. One hand set the phone recording. The other jerked the blood bag forward and squeezed it hard in his fist. A thick jet of blood squirted from the ragged hole. It sprayed over Tamoor's face and sloshed down his shirt.

He screamed out, spitting wildly, and tried to cover his face with his arm. Derrick squeezed the bag again and poured the rest of the blood over Tamoor's hair.

'I swear I'm going to kill you!' shouted Tamoor. He wiped desperately at his face. Blood dripped off his chin. His trapped arm tugged hard at the cuffs. The whole branch shuddered and creaked. Leaves tumbled down and stuck to the blood.

The air reeked of it now. The Beast would come. There was no way it would be able to resist.

'Come on, kitty!' shouted Derrick, throwing his head from side to side.

'Seriously, what is wrong with you?'

Derrick grabbed the second bag and fumbled to stab it open. Tamoor strained with all of his weight and a sharp *crack* cut through the noise of the rustling leaves. The sound of it made Derrick drop the bag.

As he ducked to retrieve it the branch gave way with a splintering *snap*. Tamoor stumbled forward and collided with him. Half of the branch trailed from his wrist. They toppled together into the grass. The mobile phone tumbled out of Derrick's grip. Derrick tried to scramble away but Tamoor had him pinned. The mound of his belly was trapped between Tamoor's knees. The first punch hit him before he saw it coming. Pain blossomed from his cheek and he screamed out in surprise. His hands covered his face automatically to block a second blow.

'You're as mental as your sister!' shouted Tamoor as he rained down punches.

A fist cracked against Derrick's elbow. Tamoor flinched and leaned back to shake out his hand. Derrick bucked his hips to try and tip him off. A punch slammed into his chest as Tamoor rode the movement and kept his balance.

'You're out here looking for monsters when you should be looking in your own house!'

Tamoor scrabbled a hand through the grass until it found the second bag of blood. He ripped it open with his teeth like an animal. Then he tipped it upside down and poured it over Derrick's face.

Blood filled his nose. It hit the back of his throat and choked off his breathing. Derrick tried to cough and splutter it clear but it just kept pouring in. It flooded his eyes and blinded his vision.

Suddenly Tamoor stood up, breathing hard. He grabbed the tree branch that dangled from his wrist and wielded it like a club. He brought it up over his head. Derrick waited for the blow to fall. Waited to feel the branch smash his skull into pieces. It didn't scare him. He realised that he didn't care at all.

Tamoor's eyes flared. Then the anger suddenly evaporated from his face. He lowered the branch and let it drop to his side.

Derrick flopped over onto his front and coughed as if his lungs were trying to evacuate his body. Blood oozed out of his nostrils. The coppery stink of it was too much to bear and he vomited. Every inch of his body heaved and trembled.

Tamoor spat and wiped at his lips. He rubbed at his wrist where the cuffs were still tightly sealed.

'I said I was sorry, didn't I?' he shouted. His voice echoed off the sheds nearby.

'You didn't mean it. You never cared about our friendship.' Derrick's voice came out weakly.

'We were friends for years!'

'You gave it up pretty quick when you found out Charlotte tried to kill herself. You didn't want anything to do with me.'

Tamoor began to walk away, then huffed and spun around. 'Is that what you think? You think it had anything to do with that?'

Derrick managed to put his knees underneath him and lift his eyes.

'I outgrew you, man,' said Tamoor. 'I wanted to do normal stuff and you were dragging me round this place looking for some imaginary panther. It was too much, man. I didn't like how you were acting.'

'Like what?'

'You blame everything on your sister! Your problems ain't her fault, and you definitely ain't the only person with problems. It made you weird, and I didn't need that. You can't *control* everything. Life don't work that way.'

Derrick flopped back onto the grass.

'I'm sorry for how things worked out,' said Tamoor. 'I didn't mean . . .'

For a moment Tamoor hovered over him as if he were trying to finish the sentence. Then he gave up, turned away and stormed across to the gate. The branch trailed after him like a pet being taken for a walk.

The grass underneath him was soaked. Derrick pulled himself slowly up onto his knees again. One hand dabbed at his aching cheek to check for blood. Then he remembered there was blood everywhere! He tipped his head back and laughter bubbled out of him. Then he shuffled to a patch of fresh grass and wiped his face across it, bent over as if in prayer.

It wouldn't be easy trying to explain why he was covered in blood when he got home. There was no way to check the damage in the darkness. He retrieved his rucksack and found his phone just under the tree. The video was still running. A swipe of his thumb left a red smear across the screen. Then he stumbled for the gate. Pain throbbed across his chest where the punch had landed.

The breeze had died and everything was completely still. Derrick knew that the Beast was close. He tried to imagine how it saw him. He must be a strange curiosity. A stupid fat kid trying to fight back against something so much bigger than himself. Something he couldn't even see, let alone understand. Even when it spoke to him it didn't seem to make any sense.

Derrick stopped in the middle of the vegetable patches. He knew it was there even if no one else could see it.

'You can't beat me!' he shouted as loudly as he could. His voice bounced off the sheds and echoed back and forth across the spread of allotments.

When Derrick tried to shout again his voice cracked. He felt his eyes grow hot, but he blinked away the tears.

'Please,' he said quietly to his feet.

A sudden breeze came from nowhere and sent a chill through his body. Derrick shivered and lifted his head. Directly ahead of him were two green lights, shining in the darkness. A single pair of eyes, without a body to call home. Derrick stared, mesmerised, and as he did, another set of ice-green rounds emerged over by the oak tree, then another pair, then more. So many eyes, in every direction, all focused unwaveringly upon him.

His heart thundered in his ears. *You're still alive*, it said. *You're still alive.*

As quickly as they had appeared, they began to vanish – one after the other in a symmetrical wave until only one pair remained. It was impossible to tell if they were right in front of him or miles in the distance.

Derrick looked dead at them. They were testing him, to see what he was made of. Derrick wouldn't look away.

You're still alive.

Then in a silent flash they, too, were gone.

Chapter Twenty

The champagne fizzed sharply on his tongue. The bubbles made him cough, but he tried to hide it. Mum and Charlotte didn't seem to notice. They were too busy clinking glasses and pawing over the letter clutched between them.

'I'm way too stupid to have got a "B" in science.'

'It's probably because I helped you,' said Derrick.

'Yeah, sure.' Charlotte flashed him a grin. It was an expression he hadn't seen on her face for a long time.

Mum sipped at her glass. 'There's still so much left to buy.'

The page had too many numbers that Derrick didn't understand. All he knew was that the lack of crying and screaming made it pretty obvious that she had got into her first-choice university. One month from now and Charlotte would be gone.

It almost felt like a victory. Almost. It wasn't a guarantee. Derrick still had to make sure she got there.

She drained her glass of champagne down in one long gulp. Mum left to grab a second bottle.

Charlotte kept reading the letter over and over. It

was as if she were scared that the results might change if she looked away. Her phone kept bleeping in her pocket as messages poured in from her friends. She ignored them.

She looked brighter than she had in months. Every few seconds the smile would threaten to disappear from her face, and just as it was about to fade it would spring back again. It was as if the muscles were too weak to hold it in place. She didn't blink. She looked shell-shocked. Her hands were shaking.

'Happy?' said Derrick.

Charlotte glanced up at him and let out a shaky breath. 'Definitely. Terrified, too.'

'I thought it's what you wanted?'

'It is,' she said, nodding uncertainly. 'But now it's happened I'm not sure it changes anything.'

Before Derrick could answer Mum stepped around the door and fired a cork inches from his face.

'Oops.'

The letter had made the house feel lighter. It was as if it had broken through the black bubble when it came through the letter box. Maybe a little bit of the real world was leaking in, or maybe some of the bad stuff was leaking out. For the first time in months it felt like things had a chance to get better.

You shouldn't count on it.

The thought hit him harder than the cork nearly had.

Last night when he got home he ran straight upstairs before anyone could see him, jumped into the shower, and stayed there for a long time. Standing there under the water, watching the dark wisps of blood disappear into the plughole, a part of him had hoped that his whole body would dissolve and let him drift away.

Early this morning he had received a text from Hadley. The phone woke him as it vibrated itself off the desk and landed with a *thud*. His cheek still throbbed like it had its own pulse. As soon as he'd swung his legs over the edge of the bed he noticed a dark bruise had spread across his chest. It disappeared into the fold under his nipple.

Part of the plan had been to win Hadley over, proving the Beast was real, avenging Tamoor's terrible behaviour towards her, impressing her with his bravery and cunning and devotion. Looking at the text message, it was fair to say that the plan . . . well, it hadn't really gone to plan.

What the hell did you think you were doing!? the text read. *Are you psycho or what?* It was only the first of a string of messages. All of them were filled with the kind of thing that TV soap characters scream at one another before someone gets their head caved in by an ashtray.

Stay away from Tamoor! And stay away from me!

The celebrations tailed off as Charlotte rang Dad to tell him the news. Derrick poured the rest of his champagne down the sink and sloped off to his room.

It wouldn't have taken Tamoor long to run off to Hadley after it happened. Derrick creaked back in his desk chair and imagined it. Tamoor storming off across the allotments as blood dripped a trail behind him. The handcuffs and tree branch scraping on the pavement as he hurried around the corner. It wouldn't have been easy to get the cuffs off. Maybe he hadn't yet. Derrick couldn't help but smile. That would certainly put a dent in their love life.

There was no anger or guilt left inside him. Now he just felt . . . empty. It was odd how nothingness, this much nothingness, could feel so much like *something*. Tamoor's words echoed through his mind. It was hard to believe that it was his fault their friendship had ended. It couldn't be true. Tamoor was just trying to shift the blame.

Derrick deleted the video he had recorded last night on his phone without bothering to play it. He couldn't bear to relive it, if he was honest. It would only show another failure.

All of those eyes shining like phosphorescence in the night had been there solely to taunt him.

He opened up his laptop to Facebook. No notifications. He scrolled down his news feed to take in the lives of his pretend online friends.

A few scrolls down was a status update from Hadley, posted only half an hour ago: *So angry!!! Going shopping with the 'rents!* The post was checked in on Croydon High Street.

Derrick stared at the screen. The anger was directed at him. That much was obvious, but the post told him something else, too – it told him Hadley's house was empty.

Slowly he closed his laptop.

Derrick paused at the end of the path. The car wasn't in the drive. He glanced around, but the street was empty.

It felt like he was doing something illicit. Slowly he walked up the path to the front door and pressed the doorbell. The electronic chimes echoed through the house. Straight away he could tell that no one was home. It was an empty sound, like a stone falling into a well. He took the spare key from his pocket and let himself in.

Beads of sweat formed on his forehead. He closed the door quickly behind him and pressed his back to it. The silence made him hold his breath, but being inside felt more natural than he had thought it would. Not just because he had been coming here his entire life. The darkness had followed him, wreathed around his shoulders like a cape.

He stepped into the sitting room. The same old pale cream sofas stared at a blank high-definition TV. Magazines were scattered across the floor. It was a room he had been into hundreds of times before. He'd always imagined what it would be like to come down here in the morning in his underwear, turn on the TV and sit cross-legged on the sofa with a bowl of cereal.

Next he wandered through into the kitchen. The fridge light blinked on when he opened the door. There were a couple of packets of fish, a whole shelf loaded with vegetables, cartons of juice, a stack of yoghurt. It was more food than they'd had at home for weeks. The inside of the door was lined with bottles of beer. Derrick took one and let the cold perspiration from the glass run over his skin. Then he decided against it and returned it to the rack.

He stood at the back door. Their garden was smaller

than his. There was no allotment behind it. The fence just divided their garden from neighbours on all sides.

That was enough time wasted. He turned and walked up the stairs.

The smell of her perfume greeted him even before he'd pushed open her bedroom door. The room had barely changed since he last stood there. The pile of clothes on the chequered sofa was a little smaller than before. A few more random objects had tumbled to the floor. The air felt warmer here than in the rest of the house. Derrick tugged at the collar of his T-shirt.

The bed was higher off the ground than normal beds. It was more like a bunk bed, but with a wardrobe built in underneath. Derrick knew he would never be invited to lie there. After all these years of telling himself that he might have had a chance, he finally knew that it had always been bullshit. It had been something he'd needed to tell himself. The hope had helped him carry on.

He pictured Tamoor's smirk. *Come on, man. Really?*

Derrick shifted his weight and kicked off the ground. When he rolled onto the bed covers discarded items of makeup dug into his back.

Perfume drifted up from the mattress like a cloud. This was where she slept. This was where she –

All he did was stick it in and lie there.

Derrick bounced his hips up and down on the mattress. The bed rocked against the wall but didn't make much noise. The wooden frame creaked a little, but not loudly enough to be heard outside the room.

The pillow felt luxuriously soft underneath his head.

Maybe somewhere in another life he was lying there with Hadley beside him. In that universe he wasn't fat. Charlotte didn't have scars on her arms and Mum was at work without having to worry about being away from home.

They had been cut off from reality for so long. They just had to last one more month. They had to help Charlotte escape to university. It was their only chance to get back to the real world.

He flipped himself over onto his front. The pillow engulfed his face. The fabric was smooth and shiny, worn down by years and years of nights beneath her head.

Derrick scooted his weight across the mattress and thumped back to the carpet. He threw open the wardrobe doors. It was practically empty, just a collection of mismatched coat hangers. Most of the clothes were piled on the sofa behind him.

He opened the drawer that sat underneath. His breath caught in his throat.

Female underwear wasn't exactly his specialist subject, but he recognised immediately the white cotton, red lace, black balls of tights. Sweat prickled all over his body. A lump slid down his throat so he could breathe again. He glanced at the door. It hung half open. The house beyond it was still encased in silence.

His fingers twitched over the drawer like he was preparing to snatch a precious artefact. Gently he pinched either end of the red lace underwear. They seemed too small to fit a real person. They were decorated with woven leaves that seemed to blow across the material as if caught in a breeze. Derrick lifted them to his lips and blew. Part of the garment was almost completely transparent. Heat flooded his cheeks.

He leaned his head forward to press his nose into the lace. It smelled of her perfume, mixed with the fresh scent of clean washing. It felt like a battering ram against his senses. Static electricity seemed to fizz over his skin.

Derrick tipped his head back and breathed them deeper. If he tried hard enough he was sure the scent could engulf him. He spread the underwear across his face. It still didn't feel close enough to his skin. Gripping them delicately by the waist he drew them back and stretched them over his head. He closed his eyes and breathed the smell deep into his lungs. The lace grated against his nose. The emptiness inside him expanded and contracted with every breath.

'What the *fuck* are you doing?'

Derrick's eyes snapped open.

The ceiling appeared above him in two red lace windows. His nose was flattened and it suddenly felt like the material would suffocate him. Slowly he turned around.

Hadley was staring at him with her mouth wide open, one hand rested on the door, the other clenched into a fist. Through the underwear windows he watched her eyebrows draw themselves down with anger.

The only thing Derrick could think to say was 'Bugger.'

'Take those off.' She kept her voice deliberately quiet. Somewhere in the back of his mind Derrick was aware that he'd always wanted her to say those words to him. In another reality they had a very different meaning. But this wasn't another reality. This was *right now*.

He snatched them off his face and winced at the sound of the delicate material tearing as it snagged on his ear. He balled them up in his hands and stepped forward hesitantly to hand them over.

'Just drop it!'

Derrick dropped the underwear like they were on fire.

'What the hell is wrong with you?'

Derrick shook his head as he considered the question. It felt like he had woken up while sleepwalking. Somehow he couldn't quite remember how he had got there. Maybe Tamoor had been telling him the truth. He didn't know when he had started behaving this way. There was no one to blame for it but himself.

Before he even knew it was coming Derrick tipped his head back and began to laugh. It doubled him over and poured wildly out of his body. The pit inside him seemed to turn itself inside out and the laughter gushed like a burst pipe.

'Derrick . . .'

'I'm sorry,' he said. He had to spit the words out through the laughter. 'It's just so ridiculous.'

'What is?'

He wiped tears from his eyes. 'Me. Everything. All of this. I just wish I'd realised it sooner.'

Laughter shuddered through his body like a gigantic sob and he buckled over again.

'Derrick, I really think we should talk. Tamoor told me you're still looking for this panther?'

She stepped forward and reached a hand out to his shoulder.

Derrick straightened up quickly to dodge the gesture. He sucked the laughter back down inside himself.

'No,' he said, adjusting his T-shirt. 'I'm sorry.'

He pushed past her and ran down the stairs onto the street.

Chapter Twenty-one

Charlotte's door was open and crappy dance music was blaring into the house. That was strange by itself. Even stranger was how she was holding different dresses against herself in the mirror. It was like he'd walked into a scene from a movie. It was so *normal*. It was the kind of sight that hadn't been welcome in this house for a long time.

She spotted him standing there and held a pair of dresses to her front. Both of them were black and looked pretty much the same to him.

'Which do you think?' she said.

'The black one.'

'Like I'd listen to you anyway.' She threw both dresses onto the bed. 'You dress like an *X Factor* reject.'

That made him smile. 'You're actually going outside?'

'I'm socially obliged to go out and celebrate my results.'

'I would have thought you'd *want* to celebrate.'

'Yeah, I thought so, too.'

'Is Mum ok with you going out?'

Charlotte looked at him like he was an idiot. 'I'm the first person in the family to ever get into university. She's ready to kick me out the door.'

'So no pressure, then.'

She looked at him for a long moment. Her eyes were full of uncertainty. Suddenly it seemed like all of this was just an attempt to hide it. A show to keep Mum happy. Derrick coughed, and couldn't hold her eye.

She leaned down to her laptop. 'How's your panther hunt going?'

He heard the amusement in her voice and tried to think how he could possibly answer. The whole thing felt like a practical joke he hadn't been let in on.

Before he could answer the music changed. A repetitive beat was replaced with a familiar steady guitar rhythm. He didn't recognise it until another guitar slammed in on top, like fists hitting a slab of meat.

It was 'Eye of the Tiger'.

'That's not funny.'

She ignored him and raised the volume, before clicking ahead to the chorus.

'...*the last known survivor stalks his prey in the night*...'

'It's not even a tiger!'

She turned to face him and banged her head along to the rhythm. Derrick burst out laughing. It was the most animated he'd seen her in as long as he could remember.

He huffed exaggeratedly and went into his room, closing the door behind him. The music thumped through the wall. He kept laughing. It was all so ridiculous. It had taken him this long to realise it.

They weren't safe yet. He knew that they could all feel it. Charlotte getting the results she needed was one thing. There was still a long way to go before they were out of the woods.

The music fell quiet. He banged on the wall to try and encourage her to turn it back on. The silence suddenly felt like too much to bear.

When the doorbell rang later that night, Derrick hid in his room. It could have been Hadley. It wasn't just that he didn't want to be around her. He *definitely* didn't want to be around if she spoke to his family. There was no way that conversation could go well.

Too many voices reverberated up the stairs for it to be just Hadley. The sound of girly laughter reached him. Charlotte's friends. Judging by the volume of screeching going on it was probably fair to say that they had all passed their exams too – another good reason to stay hidden. It must have been months since her friends last came round to visit. He wondered if they felt it when they walked through the door. The oppressive atmosphere that leaned its weight on them constantly.

Charlotte going out. That was something else that hadn't happened for months.

She had chosen one of the black dresses in the end. It didn't hide the scars on her arms and legs, or the bandage that still covered her wrist.

When he heard the front door slam Derrick ventured downstairs. As usual, Mum had immediately camped in front of the news.

'That was some efficient hiding.'

'Thanks. They're gone, right?'

'They're actually behind the sofa.'

Derrick smirked and slumped down next to her. The news was playing sports footage. It was the first time in weeks he'd seen it when it wasn't shouting about some disaster. Maybe it was a sign.

As if she had read his mind Mum lifted the remote and muted the TV. 'I've got a fun activity for this evening.'

'When you say "fun" . . .?'

'We're going to sort out the stuff Charlotte's taking to university with her.'

Derrick frowned. 'She's not moving for another four weeks.'

'I'm her mother. I've been preparing for this for months.'

Derrick supposed that he had been too.

She switched off the TV and pushed herself to her feet. Derrick sighed and sprawled himself across the sofa. He felt his flesh spread underneath him like an airbed.

Mum lifted an eyebrow and pointed at the door.

'Ugh, fine,' said Derrick. He struggled upright and followed her into the hall.

They traipsed up the stairs and into her bedroom. For just a second, before she switched the light on, he caught a glimpse of the darkened allotments outside the window.

Mum opened up the wardrobe. A bunch of pots and pans spilled out onto her feet.

'The stockpile has how reached critical mass.'

'So this is why you had to put the knives back downstairs.'

They took out the collection of household objects one by one and piled them on the floor. The pots and pans were joined by fresh towels, a box of Ikea cutlery, a new iPhone dock, a pouch of toiletries, and a bag of food in jars and tins.

'Feel free to tell me if I've forgotten anything,' she said as she handed him a wall calendar for next year. Every month featured a different picture of a kitten wearing a jumper.

'Mum, you have enough to stock a fallout shelter.'

The next step was to checklist everything. Derrick wondered if where Charlotte was moving to didn't have shops or the Internet. Mum stood in the middle of the mess and ticked each item off a list.

Ever since it had been confirmed that Charlotte would attend university it seemed to have given Mum fresh purpose. She still looked exhausted – it would practically take a coma to fix her kind of tiredness – but it no longer looked like she might collapse under it at any moment. She looked like she was on the final stretch of a marathon. She looked like she'd make the finish line. She looked like she was in control again.

Derrick sat on the edge of the bed. 'She'll be ok, won't she?'

'Not if I forget something.'

'No, I mean, she'll be ok away from home?'

Mum peered at him over the top of the list. It hid the dark circles under her eyes. 'She's not exactly been happy here.'

Derrick frowned. None of them had exactly been happy here. Not for a long time.

'We've all been assuming it'll be better for her away from home,' said Derrick. 'But what if it isn't?'

Mum threw the list into the wardrobe and perched beside him on the bed. 'She can't stay here for ever. The fact that she feels positive about moving is a huge step forward. And she can come home whenever she wants.'

'You mean I can't turn her room into a man cave?'

'No, dear. We need to do our best to support her from a distance.'

Derrick ran his eyes over the selection of household objects spread across the carpet. It was like staring at a brand-new life broken down to its smallest components. It would be a huge step for anyone to take. It had seemed so obvious before – get her to university and everything would be ok. But Charlotte had struggled so much just living at home. It seemed impossible that she would cope on her own.

'She told me she was scared.'

Mum shook her head thoughtfully. 'I'm not surprised. It petrifies me.'

She stretched an arm around his shoulder. He leaned into her. It would just be the two of them for the next couple of years. It would be better here for them. The depression would be banished and their house would reconnect with the rest of the world. It would be a new beginning.

The phone shrilled up the stairs to break the silence between them.

'Phone,' said Derrick.

'I'll get it, shall I?' Mum withdrew her arm and tipped him back onto the bed. Then she hurried out of the room. Derrick listened to her feet creak to the bottom of the stairs.

When he heard the ringing stop he pulled himself up to his feet. He picked his way through the assorted mess and ducked under the net curtains. The only way to see the allotments through the glare of the overhead light was to press his face against the glass.

They were as still as they always were. There was no sign of a breeze tonight. The shadow of the oak sat stoically in the dim light. It was like a sentry standing watch over the sheds and vegetables and the broken swing set. Somehow it had always felt like the oak tree was on his side.

Derrick wondered if anyone had found the blood spattered across the grass. That would give anyone a shock. His eyes glanced up at the black expanse of the sky. He half expected to see a helicopter buzz overhead. Just like all those nights ago.

In the darkness there was no way to make out the cage. There was no sign of the Beast. Somehow he had to keep it away from them for the next month. It would be easier now. That's what he had to tell himself.

The stairs creaked behind him. Derrick turned away from the window, quickly replaced the net curtains and stumbled over a pile of books. He was standing in the middle of it all when Mum stepped through the door. The phone was clutched tight to her chest. She stared at him with eyes that were wide and shimmering. A shiver ran its fingers up Derrick's spine.

She opened her mouth to speak.

Chapter Twenty-two

The next few hours were a strange parade of pointless details. Derrick's brain seemed to switch itself off. It only broke the surface now and again to take a snapshot of life.

The car stopped at traffic lights. Derrick didn't remember getting into the passenger seat. A van rumbled across the junction ahead of them. Mum gripped the steering wheel as if it were the only thing that held the car together.

A phone in his hand. Somewhere on the other end was Dad's voice. Derrick realised with a jolt of horror that it had somehow fallen to him to break the news.

'Dad,' he said.

The hospital entrance was lit up like a beacon. They hurried inside. The entrance hall was a wide-open space decorated with potted plants and posters about hygiene. Makeup ran from the eyes of Charlotte's friends like black tears. Their parents crowded around Mum. No one spoke to him.

He tugged at the hem of his T-shirt.

Derrick's brain seemed to latch on to these details

because they were simple and easy to focus on. They made sense, until he tried to relate them to what was actually happening – then his mind would slip back into darkness and all thought vanished until another detail would suddenly pull him back, as if trying to save him from the brink of unconsciousness.

Every time he came back the same thought hit him. *This is real. You can't pretend. This is happening to you.*

It still didn't feel like it.

The hospital walls probably used to be white. Now they looked faded, marked with dark scuffs along the paintwork. Pictures lined the walls, of people who must be hospital staff. A man in blue smiled, a miniature watch clipped upside down to his pocket. A young woman in green had her hair hacked short. There was an older woman in a chef's hat.

Double doors opened in front of him. A thin woman with thick glasses and a red jumper stopped them. Derrick looked at his shoes while she spoke to Mum. He wondered how he would feel about this tomorrow. In fifty years. He wondered if he would feel guilty for all the pointless crap he had noticed on the way here.

Eventually a deep breath made Mum's shoulders tremble. Her whole body seemed to deflate, like the doctor had punctured her.

They stood at a door. It had a square window, blocked off inside by a white blind.

Finally someone spoke to Derrick. 'Are you sure you want to see her?'

Suddenly it was real.

*

Derrick had believed that things were getting better. It hadn't been a complete victory, he hadn't won anything, but the exam results had felt like a fresh dose of hope – just enough to keep the darkness from destroying them entirely.

He remembered her in front of the mirror. One by one she had held different dresses against her skinny body. Maybe there had been more to that moment than he had been able to see. Maybe it had been a more significant choice than anyone could have guessed.

Derrick sat stiffly in the front passenger seat of the car. He looked out across the car park. Even at this time of night it was packed with other vehicles. The owners must all have been trapped inside the hospital.

He had needed to escape. The hospital was equipped with designated 'quiet areas', small rooms with sofas and magazines. He had been left alone in one. It hadn't been quiet at all. They were packed with people, coming and going, chatting loudly and crying. Alerts blared out along the hospital corridors. Trolleys banged against the walls. The car was the only place he had been able to think of that would be, genuinely, quiet.

He pictured what he'd seen inside Charlotte's hospital room. The edges of her dress hanging over the bed. He knocked his head hard against the side window to snuff it out.

She had done it at somebody else's house. That was the one part of it he couldn't understand – the depression smothered *their* house, a few other places nearby. That was where it pushed against you, made terrible things happen. He thought she was on the road to escape. He didn't know it would mean *this*.

It shocked him that this was the only detail he struggled to understand. Nothing else made him feel surprised or horrified. He wasn't crying. He hadn't collapsed at her bedside and refused to leave. He was sitting alone in the car.

Instead, a strange sense of inevitability had hung over him ever since he'd heard the news. It was like when his grandparents had died – it wasn't exactly unexpected. It felt as if, somewhere deep inside himself, he had been prepared for this night all along.

But still he didn't know how to feel.

His phone vibrated in his pocket. He hadn't even remembered he had it with him.

He swiped the cracked screen to life. It was a text from Hadley: *We've just heard. I'm so sorry. Are you ok??x*

Derrick stared at the screen. He stared even when the light had blinked off. The news had already spread. All of Charlotte's friends would have spilled it to everyone they knew by now. It would be in text messages, emails, Tweets. Her Facebook profile would already be nothing but a memorial.

Shame burned his cheeks.

He shoved the phone back into his pocket without sending a reply.

The driver's door creaked open. Dad slumped down into the seat and thumped the door closed. A gust of cool air needled Derrick's skin.

'Hi.'

Derrick kept his eyes on the windscreen. 'How long have you been here?'

'Half an hour or so. I've just been inside.'

His eyes were rimmed red. He'd been crying. Derrick had never even imagined that his dad could cry.

They sat in silence for a few minutes. Blue ambulance lights flashed from the front of the hospital out over and around the car park. The noise of the siren barely managed to reach them.

'Is Mum ok?'

'She's still with the doctor.'

'I didn't mean to leave her on her own.'

Dad leaned his head back against the headrest. 'Don't worry. I'm sure she understands.'

Derrick turned to look across at his father. His eyes were absent, he stared out of the window unseeing. Maybe he had needed to escape the hospital too. Derrick wondered if everyone else in the family had been secretly prepared for this night.

'I need to pee,' said Derrick.

Dad turned and blinked at him. 'Follow me.'

The car doors thudded closed behind them. Their footsteps on the tarmac echoed gently between the other cars. Dad led the way as they weaved between the caged trees that divided the car park into sections. The only other people nearby were gathered around the hospital doors. Smoke drifted off them like a weather front.

They found a dark corner out of view, where an outbuilding met a graffiti-scrawled concrete wall.

'Here should be all right.'

Derrick glanced over his shoulder towards the hospital. Dad followed his gaze. Then he shrugged and opened his flies to step up to the wall.

After another glance back, Derrick stepped up beside him. This was the last thing he should be scared about.

A steady splashing sound filled the air between them.

'Were you all right in there?' said Dad.

Derrick looked down at the dark stain that spread outwards down the wall. 'Better than I should have been.'

'You don't need to be anything. Did it scare you?'

Derrick looked across to nod, before he remembered what they were doing. He redirected his eyes forward. 'Yeah.'

Dad bounced on his feet before he resealed his fly. 'I'm trying to think of it like this,' he said. 'Charlotte was depressed, but she didn't want to be. That's why this happened. She wouldn't want us to feel unhappy because of her decision.'

Something caught in Derrick's throat. He heaved in a breath and tears welled up in his eyes. He blinked them away while he shook himself and rearranged his jogging bottoms. The decision should have been hers. But what if the depression didn't give her a choice? There would never be a way to find out.

Dad put a hand on his shoulder. Derrick saw his lip tremble. Both of them sucked in a breath at the same time, forcing themselves not to cry. Forcing themselves to stay in control.

Dad pulled him into a hug, and they stayed that way for a while.

'I've already missed so much time with her.'

'I think we all did.'

They were silent for a moment.

'Did you ever think about doing it?' Derrick said into his shoulder.

There was a long shuddering breath before the answer came. 'Sometimes. I was always too frightened.'

'She wasn't weak, was she?'

'She was probably stronger than any of us.'

Derrick pulled away. 'You've pissed on your shoes,' he said, pointing at wet splashes on Dad's trainers.

'Bugger.'

Dad found a patch of weeds a little further along the wall and scraped the top of his feet through it, swiping back and forth until he was satisfied.

'Better?'

'Yeah.'

'Should we go and find your mum?'

Derrick gazed across at the hospital building. It seemed like every window blazed with light. There were thousands upon thousands of them. Every window was lit up by an individual tragedy. The whole building seemed to glow with it. Derrick shoved his hands into his pockets.

'Yeah, let's go.'

Derrick remembered a dream he'd had once about coming back to the house after something like this had happened to Charlotte. In the dream he had hesitated at the door. Blinked like an amnesiac when the lights came on. He had wandered aimlessly around the house like a spectre.

When they opened the front door Mum walked straight through to the kitchen. All the lights were still on. The cat moaned from the windowsill outside to be let indoors. When Derrick opened the door she jumped onto the table and looked at them, expecting attention. Cool air from the garden drifted into the room.

Derrick breathed and it felt easier, freer, than it had done for months. A weight had been lifted. The black bubble had burst. Traces of it would linger in the house for months, maybe longer, but he knew the atmosphere had changed. It didn't feel like they were caught in a trap any more. It felt like they were back in the real world, whether they wanted it or not.

This was what he had wanted, what he had fought for; in the end, he had to lose the person he'd been fighting for in the first place.

He had no idea what he was supposed to do next.

Mum put the kettle on. 'Tea?'

Derrick shook his head. He sat at the table and ran his hands down the cat's back. Mum excused herself to use the toilet. She looked tiny. She reminded him of the ornaments in Charlotte's room, dashed against the wall and broken into countless pieces.

The kettle began to gargle. Derrick stared at the table. The emptiness inside him was gone. It was as if it had been tied to the darkness, as if they couldn't exist without each other. There was something else there now. Something he couldn't quite grasp.

After a few minutes Mum still hadn't come back downstairs. He made a mug of tea, trying to keep the cat hair on his hands from falling into it, and took it upstairs.

'Mum.'

She was sitting on the edge of her bed, surrounded by the things that Charlotte would never take to university. Now it seemed like detritus washed ashore from a shipwreck. Derrick handed her the mug and sat beside her.

Mum took a slow sip of tea.

Derrick felt something flicker in his stomach. 'Why did this happen?'

The mug stayed halfway to her mouth. For just a second her eyebrows crumpled. But she forced them back up, like scaffolding supporting a condemned building.

Derrick willed himself to keep his eyes on her. 'I don't understand why she did it. Everything was getting better. I mean, I know it doesn't *get better*, but she seemed ok. She passed her exams, and she was going to university. That's everything she wanted. I just don't . . .'

Mum gave him as much time as he needed to find the right words.

'I just don't get why she did it.'

The corners of her mouth tightened into a joyless smile. 'I don't have an answer for you,' she said. 'I'm sorry, but there *isn't* a good answer. We can't understand – not properly. That's the nature of the beast.'

Derrick swallowed hard. His eyes turned

automatically to the window. There was nothing to see but the room reflected back at them.

'She promised me,' he said, eyes still on the window. 'She promised me she wouldn't do it.'

'I know she did. But you can't blame her for not keeping that promise.'

Derrick nodded. There would be enough blame for them all to share. They would all harbour it for the rest of their lives, trying to store as much of it for themselves as they could manage.

Mum looked at the things scattered around them. 'What do you think I was holding when she did it?'

'It doesn't matter. None of this matters.'

Suddenly Mum arched her arm and hurled the mug against the wall. It exploded into shards, tea spraying across the carpet. Before there was a moment to think she was on her feet and grabbing a plate from the university stash. It smashed against the wardrobe. Then her hands found the desk lamp and she snapped it clean in two over her knee.

Derrick was on his feet too. The first thing in his hands was a cooking pan and he threw it as hard as he could against the wall. Then he found a plate and watched it shatter as he stamped his full weight down on it.

Food sprayed over them as the jars burst, and they threw the fresh towels into the spreading puddles. They tore the pages from the books and scattered them. Bottles of soap and shampoo leaked into the socks and over the crushed iPod dock. Cutlery shimmered in the light as it fell and clattered over the mess.

When they had destroyed it all they stood breathing hard. It felt as if they had broken a piece of the future. A future that had never existed in the first place, no matter how hard they had tried to make it real.

Mum kicked out one last time and then began to cry. Her shoulders shuddered, and her whole body seemed to erupt with it. Derrick tried to pull her into a hug but she staggered past him, tripping over the mess and out onto the landing. She threw open Charlotte's door and collapsed onto her bed, the crumpled sheets muffling her tears.

'Mum,' said Derrick.

She roared into the bed, wringing the duvet in her fists. Derrick stood on the landing and watched. What was he supposed to do? *You should know.* But he didn't. He didn't have any idea at all how he was supposed to act.

One hand rested on his stomach. The emptiness inside had disappeared. And as Mum's cries began to dampen he realised what had replaced it. A ghost of the darkness had settled inside him. It had replaced the anger and guilt that had filled him to the brim. It would be with him for ever.

Mum's body sagged and she fell silent, the exhaustion pushing her over the brink of sleep. Derrick walked quickly down the stairs, opened the front door and slipped quietly out onto the street.

Chapter Twenty-three

It was still a few hours until the sun would rise. Street-lights drenched the road with a thick orange glow. It was the coldest part of the night. Goose pimples prickled across his arms. A patch of stars peered down at him before the clouds shifted to blot them out.

Mum's words echoed in his head. *That's the nature of the beast.*

No one was to blame for this. Derrick saw it clearly for the first time in his life. Nothing had caused this to happen. He could not have stopped it. There were no hidden secrets beyond his control.

That's the nature of the beast.

The Beast.

He didn't know what else he could do. It had meant everything to him. He couldn't just let it go.

He listened to his feet strike the pavement. When the tarmac turned to dirt underneath his trainers, the darkness between the houses closed around him.

'Derrick!'

He stopped in the middle of the track and turned back towards the road. Heavy breaths heaved in his lungs. Two figures appeared at the top of the track. The light behind them reduced them to nothing but shadows. Their feet scraped in the dirt as they jogged towards him.

Derrick stood rigidly. Hadley reached him first, followed by Tamoor.

'We caught you,' she said, her voice thin and out of breath.

Derrick took a moment to look between the two of them. 'Caught me?'

'We thought you'd be coming this way,' said Tamoor.

Derrick raised his eyebrows.

'Well, *she* knew you'd be coming. I just sort of agreed that it made sense.'

Hadley squeezed his arm. 'I'm so sorry.'

For the second time that night Derrick felt a flush of embarrassment. Pity was the last thing on his mind. There would be time to mourn later, the rest of his life would be spent in mourning, and tomorrow would be about working out how that felt. Right now he just wanted to cling to the only thing he had left.

'Everything you said about Charlotte and this panther,' said Hadley. She tugged her hoodie closer around herself. 'I just knew you'd be out here tonight. We want to help.'

Derrick glanced down towards the allotment gate. The metal and chain-link were barely visible. He turned back to look at Tamoor, and then at Hadley.

'Help me with what?'

'Whatever it is you need to do.'

Derrick didn't say another word. He turned and set

off for the gate. After a few seconds he heard their foot-steps follow behind. Any other night Derrick would have thought this was a set-up. But not tonight.

The light was a little better down by the gate. A security light blazed up from a nearby back garden. Derrick wedged a foot into the chain-link.

'I stole your dad's key,' he said. The muscles in his leg strained as he pulled himself up. He thumped down on the other side. 'I've left it at home. Sorry.'

'We just thought he was going senile,' said Hadley before she clambered up the metal.

When everyone was inside they set off together across the allotments. This was the latest he had ever been there. At this hour there wasn't much light from the nearby houses. All the windows were nothing but black squares.

The air was easier, just like at home; but, just like at home, the darkness had left its mark. The Beast was not gone.

'So this thing is definitely out here, yeah?' said Tamoor, a quiver of fear in his voice.

There was no way Derrick could prove it. It had been that way since they first searched for it three months ago. The Beast always kept itself hidden from him in ways that seemed impossible. He just had a feeling that tonight would be different. It had to be.

'What's the plan?' said Tamoor.

'It'll find me.'

'And you're not a bit . . . worried?'

Derrick shrugged. 'It wouldn't be the worst thing to happen to me tonight.'

They walked around the vegetable patches towards the oak tree. Behind him they whispered to each other like kids at the back of a classroom.

'I've never been here at night,' said Tamoor.

'Anyone would think you're starting to believe in it,' whispered Hadley.

'I don't know, man. Do you?'

Hadley didn't answer.

Derrick was glad that they were out here with him. It felt right somehow. It didn't bother him that they were here as a couple. They were the kind of constant he needed right now. They had been a part of this all along and it seemed to fit that they'd be here at the end.

Somehow the oak tree managed to cast a long shadow into the darkness. It was hard to tell, but he was sure that he could still make out blood stains in the grass. A white gash glared from the smaller tree where its arm had been torn loose.

Derrick pointed into the bushes at the dark square of the cage.

'That's yours,' he said.

Hadley peered beyond his finger. 'I wondered about that.'

Derrick dropped his arm and waded into the bushes. The branches snagged his clothes and clawed at his skin. The undergrowth crackled beneath him like a bonfire.

'Is that a good idea, man?' said Tamoor.

Derrick kept going until he reached the cage. He leaned down to check inside. The mesh was as empty as it had always been. The rotten steaks were gone. The only smell now was mud and grass. Derrick pushed on further until he reached the back fence. The crate still rested against the wood. He heaved it around to expose the open panel and peered inside. Nothing. The dark expanse of overgrowth stretched out ahead of him. He studied the leaves and weeds, the piles of abandoned junk for anything that might have changed. It was difficult to tell in the dark, but nothing struck him as different. There was no sign that the Beast had been here since it had pounced on him.

'Anything?' shouted Hadley.

Derrick shook his head. At the same moment a low growl rumbled out of the darkness. It was a noise so deep that it was little more than a vibration. It juddered through his stomach and sent a shiver cascading through his body.

'You hear that?'

At the edge of the bushes Hadley and Tamoor fell quiet, craned their necks to pick up the sound. Derrick turned his head slowly. He couldn't tell where the growl had come from. The bushes around him were dead still.

'I don't hear anything,' said Hadley, her voice shaking. 'Derrick?'

Derrick raised a hand to quiet her. His skin had begun to prickle. He imagined it like a cat's fur puffing into a ball when it senses trouble.

He turned his body towards the oak tree and the growl rumbled again. It was louder this time. Derrick snapped his head around. It had come from behind him. He lifted his hands automatically as if he'd have to fight.

'What is it?' said Hadley.

A bush shuddered just a few feet from where Derrick stood. As soon as he locked his eyes on it the leaves fell still. It was only as he waited that he heard the soft crunch of something moving through the undergrowth. A twig snapped.

Here.

'Forget this!' shouted Tamoor.

Derrick whipped around to glare at him and lifted a hand to try and keep him quiet. The light of a phone blinked up in Tamoor's hand. He fumbled in a short number and lifted it to his ear.

'Don't!' shouted Derrick.

The leaves in front of him exploded and a shape burst out and away from him. It rippled through the bushes like a torpedo through water.

Derrick didn't hesitate. He launched after it as branches beat against his legs. The ground crackled and shifted under his feet but he kept his eyes up and followed the quaking overgrowth. It pushed away from him towards the far end of the allotments.

'Derrick!' Hadley shouted after him.

Every breath burned in his lungs. The shape moved faster underneath the bushes than Derrick could barrel through them. Nettles stung his hands and arms but he didn't let it bother him.

As they reached the end of the allotments a mound of scrap wood rose up out of the bushes. Derrick saw it early and changed direction. He cut diagonally so that he emerged onto the grass. Now he could run faster, even though pain had gripped tight around his legs.

His eyes stuck on the woodpile. A black shape sprang out of the overgrowth and scrambled up and over it. It was only there for a second before it slid once again out of sight, but it was enough for Derrick to see the muscular limbs. A white shimmer of light reflecting off a sleek black coat. The long tail that trailed behind it.

The fence between the allotments and the warehouse stopped him from running any further. Every breath now was so laboured that it came out of his body like a moan. The bushes that grew right up to the fence were completely still.

For a moment Derrick stood on the grass and stared up at the roof of the warehouse. From somewhere in the sky there came a high pitched buzzing. It was a noise he recognised instantly. The *thrum* of helicopter blades as they bounced off the nearby roofs.

Derrick dived head-first into the bushes. He groped along on all fours, using one hand to clear the way ahead of him until the fence appeared like a solid wall. The wood felt damp against his fingertips. He rested on his knees and pawed at it. It had been a long time since he had last come through here. A bubble of panic swelled in his chest.

It had to be here.

The sharp edges of the jagged wood cut into his fingers. The hole was still there. He tried to work out its size but it was impossible to tell. He guessed that it was big enough. Derrick shoved his weight forward. The fence rattled as it caught on his shoulders. He wriggled them through. The edges of the hole were spongy with damp and they crumbled away. He felt the softness of his belly sag down over the wood. One long breath emptied his lungs. The wood grazed his skin and the whole fence shook and complained as he squeezed himself through. It wouldn't be a graceful entrance. His stomach cleared the hole with a jolt and he scrambled his legs after it. More leaves slapped against his face as he scrabbled forward until the earth turned to concrete underneath his hands.

From somewhere behind him he faintly heard Hadley shout his name, quickly drowned out by the din of the helicopter. The noise slammed into him directly instead of bouncing from the surrounding houses. Tamoor must have called the police.

It was just like the first night he had encountered the Beast.

It meant he had to move quickly.

Derrick jogged around the corner of the warehouse to the courtyard. Orange light from the street bathed the path ahead. It hurled his shadow ahead of him as he stepped inside the metal shell. In here the noise of the approaching helicopter sounded like a heavy chant. It was almost enough to disguise a light *thud* against the metal. Derrick turned to face the back entrance. He ducked quickly through it.

The fence blocked his way once again, but Derrick turned to the old toilet block directly beside him and, as lightly as he could, he stepped into the doorway. He saw the dirty white toilet. The old tank hung loose from the ceiling.

He was met with a thunderous growl that quaked inside his chest. Crouched against the rear wall, retreated as far as the space would allow, was the Beast.

A pair of green eyes glowered at him. The outline of the creature seemed to paint itself into existence around them. A thick, rounded snout curled up into a snarl. Its body was coiled like a spring. Muscles flexed beneath fur as black as ink. A pair of sharp shoulder blades protruded from the base of its neck. Every inch of it was tensed, sat back on its haunches and ready to pounce.

'I see you,' said Derrick. 'I see you.'

He rested a hand on the doorway to steady himself. This was the creature he had hunted for so long. This was the agent of depression that he had sought to destroy. And now he had it cornered. Derrick allowed his gaze to sink into those perfect green points of light. The Beast was as dark as a shadow. Unknowable in every way imaginable.

Slowly, Derrick turned his head away. He knew that it wouldn't make a move on him. That wasn't how this was supposed to go. It was his choice now. Over the allotment fence he saw the red lights blink on the body of the chopper. A shaft of white light beamed down from its belly. It swung back and forth over the allotments and swooped rapidly towards the warehouse. Derrick pictured Hadley and Tamoor outlined in its light, waving it on to where they had seen him disappear.

Derrick turned back to the Beast, locked eyes. It uttered a low growl from deep within. He couldn't hear it but he felt it in his gut. The growl died away, and he saw the panther's tongue. It was an obscenely bright pink, clamped between a set of sharp white fangs.

'You're trapped,' said Derrick.

The Beast lowered its head, as if in submission.

This was everything he had wanted. He stared at it, his enemy, his salvation, pinned back in the darkness and at his mercy.

'I still don't think I understand.'

The voice seemed to be inside his mind. *That is my nature.*

The helicopter's beam bounced off the panther's eyes. Derrick struggled to breathe. No one but him could decide what happened next. Finally, after all of it, the future was in his hands. Tomorrow he would have to find a way to begin his life again, emptied of everything that had propped it up for so long.

The Beast spoke to him. *You don't need me any more.*

Their eyes met. Derrick took a ragged breath. Then he stepped aside to open a gap in the broken doorway.

'Go.'

In one swift movement the Beast slipped lithely past him. Its muscles rippled beneath its coat. Soft fur brushed against Derrick's leg. It moved as quickly as an apparition. It took no more than a second for it to reach the bushes. It was impossible to tell if it was the leaves or the night itself that swallowed it up.

It was gone.

At last, he cried. Tears welled up and flooded down his face. It was the greatest sense of relief he had ever felt, as if his body had needed it for a very long time.

The spotlight found him. He dropped to his knees.

Acknowledgements

Much of the thanks for this book's existence must be given to my mum. Through countless speech therapy and home-reading sessions she pulled my woeful childhood literacy abilities up by the bootstraps. I couldn't recite the alphabet or hold a pen properly. Now I have published a book.

My dad, too, has rarely missed an opportunity to shove a book into my hands (it helps that he owns more than most libraries). Both parents, in their respective manners, instilled in me an implacable love of books and continue to be the best kind of enablers.

Christina, my sister, still puts up with me despite my relentless poor treatment of her.

Nigel and Paul, my best friends, inexplicably humour and support me at every turn, which means more to me than they will ever know. They are also experts in cutting me down to size when required, which is often.

I couldn't hope for better friends than Miggy, Junaid, Ritch, and Sam, who somehow don't seem offended by my continuing presence in their lives.

Mr Illingworth was the kind of inspirational English teacher I thought only existed in fiction. Thanks to him I never feel too pusillanimous to promulgate my loquacious vocabulary.

Judy Waite and Judith Heneghan, my mentors at the University of Winchester, gave me their invaluable guidance, showed me that this was possible, and never told me my ideas were stupid (even when they were).

Ella, my agent, is ruthlessly talented at combining kind words and keen criticism. She made this book happen.

Sarah, my editor, understood this book even better than I did.

Lastly, everyone at Constable & Robinson. You cats are all right.